GENTLEMEN
PREFER BLONDES

THE
ILLUMINATING DIARY
OF A PROFESSIONAL LADY

By

ANITA LOOS

Intimately Illustrated by

RALPH BARTON

WITH THE
INTRODUCTORY ESSAY
*The Jazz Age Literature of
the Lost Generation*

First published in 1925

Read &' Co.

Copyright © 2021 Read & Co. Classics

This edition is published by Read & Co. Classics,
an imprint of Read & Co.

This book is copyright and may not be reproduced in any
way without the express permission of the publisher in writing.

British Library Cataloguing-in-Publication Data
A catalogue record for this book is available
from the British Library.

Read & Co. is part of Read Books Ltd.
For more information visit
www.readandcobooks.co.uk

TO
JOHN EMERSON

CONTENTS

ILLUSTRATIONS

———————

8

ANITA LOOS

Corinne Anita Loos was born in California on 26th April 1888. A talented American playwright, screenwriter, and novelist, she is best known for her dauntless novel, *Gentlemen Prefer Blondes* (1925), later produced as a Hollywood blockbuster of the same name, starring Marylin Monroe (1952).

From a young age, Loos was her family's leading source of income. At six, she began performing in local productions, including with her father's theatre company. In 1912, her first screenplay, *The New York Hat*, was produced as a silent short film, directed by D. W. Griffith and starring Mary Pickford and Lionel Barrymore.

In 1915, Loos married the son of a band conductor, Frank Pallma, Jr. After six months of marriage, she realised that Pallma had little money and was no match for her quick wit. One day, while he was running an errand, she packed her bags and left. The same year, after her screenplay's success, Griffith hired Loos as a scriptwriter for the Triangle Film Corporation. He invited her to collaborate with him and Frank E. Woods for the epic *Intolerance* (1916). After travelling to New York City for the film's premiere, Loos decided to spend the autumn in the city. Here, she met American journalist Frank Crowninshield and continued to contribute articles to his new magazine, *Vanity Fair*, for several decades.

On her return to California, Loos joined Griffith and fellow screenwriter John Emerson in collaboration on five Douglas Fairbanks films, which helped the actor rise to fame. When Fairbanks was offered a deal with the motion picture company Famous Players-Lasky, he took the Emerson-Loos team with him.

In 1918, Famous Players-Lasky offered the team a four-picture deal in New York. Emerson and Loos moved into a mansion on Long Island together. There, they wrote *Getting Mary Married* for William Randolph Hearst's mistress, Marion Davies, which was released in 1919. The two continued to work together, writing *A Temperamental Wife* (1919) and *A Virtuous Vamp* (1919) for their friend and independent producer, Constance Talmadge. Emerson and Loos then moved into the Ambassador Hotel on Park Avenue, where their friends the Talmadges and the Schencks lived.

Later that year, Loos filed for divorce from her first husband and married Emerson on the Schenck estate on 15th June 1919. The couple wrote five films in 16 months and two books on writing in 1920 and 1921. After moving into an apartment in Murray Hill, NY, they cut back to writing two films a year to spend more time travelling. *The Perfect Woman* (1920) was their final film with Schenck and Talmadge as Emerson had decided it was time to move into the theatre. Their first play, *The Whole Town's Talking*, opened at the Bijou Theatre on 29th August 1923.

Emerson persuaded Loos that he needed to take a break from their marriage once a week to date other women. To fill the heartache of her husband's absence, she became good friends with H. L. Mencken. On a train journey in 1925, she watched as he became incredibly flustered by an attractive blonde woman in the dining car. She wrote a sketch about the comical event, which formed the basis of her novel *Gentlemen Prefer Blondes* (1925).

Starring a highly-strung, ambitious flapper woman, *Gentlemen Prefer Blondes* is a comedic novel set in the Jazz Age. The novel was first released as a series of sketches in a fashion magazine, *Harper's Bazaar*. With high public demand and a push from Mencken, Loos published the satirical stories in book form. The book's first printing sold out overnight and became a 1925 bestseller. In the Spring of 1926, Loos finished writing a stage adaptation of the book, which ran for 201 performances on Broadway and the first film adaptation came out in 1928. She released a sequel to her smash hit novel, But Gentlemen Marry Brunettes, in 1927. Although the 1928 film was unsuccessful, a musical version of the book opened on Broadway in 1946 and ran for 90 weeks before a successful tour. This led to the production of a musical film version in 1953, starring Jane Russell and Marilyn Monroe, which earnt $5.3 million at the box office worldwide.

Despite a long and unhappy marriage to Emerson—one full of numerous affairs on his behalf—she had an extraordinarily successful screenwriting career throughout the first half of the twentieth century. By the 1960s, Loos began writing her memoirs. *A Girl Like I* was published in 1966, followed by *Twice Over Lightly: New York Then and Now* (1972) and *Kiss Hollywood Good-by* (1974).

On 18th August 1981, after a lengthy lung infection, Loos suffered a heart attack at Manhattan's Doctors Hospital in New York City and passed away at 93 years old, leaving a powerful legacy in her wake.

Anita Loos led an abundant professional life, with her name attached to numerous screenplays, stage productions, and books. Her career in American film stretched across 30 years, contributing over 150 screenplays to the silent film era. She was known as the life of every party, a glittering American socialite with remarkable talent.

THE JAZZ AGE
LITERATURE OF THE
LOST GENERATION

The Jazz Age is one of the most significant cultural movements in American history. Coinciding with the Roaring Twenties, the Prohibition Era, and women being granted the right to vote, the era that spanned from the First World War up to the Wall Street Crash in 1929 was a period of considerable social reform. The war had displaced thousands of Americans, with people not only losing loved ones but also their sense of purpose and direction in life. With a generation reeling from such devastation, life following the war was one of optimism, full of hope and determination for a better future. It allowed the young people to rebel against the traditional ideals that came before, exploring new artistic endeavours that helped shape a new glittering and prosperous society. Eventually becoming known as the Lost Generation, it was this wave of young people who helped form the Jazz Age of 1920s post-war America.

While the period of The Lost Generation is commonly known as America's liberating Jazz Age, jazz music had been around for many decades before then. The swinging genre of jazz began in New Orleans, Louisiana, in the late nineteenth century, with its roots in ragtime and blues. The expressive, rhythmic music originated in the pain and oppression of slavery in the United States. Black-American communities popularised the music in the early 1920s during the prohibition of alcohol. It was popular in illegal speakeasies and became a widespread genre with the rise of radio, rebelling against the traditional, popular music of the time. Jazz came to represent a sense of freedom for the people of a country devastated by oppression, war, and loss, and formed the soundtrack for the hedonistic culture of the Roaring Twenties.

Despite the era's culture being grounded in music, many prolific literary figures belonged to the Lost Generation, including the likes of F. Scott Fitzgerald and Ernest Hemingway. A term first coined by American writer Gertrude Stein and popularised by Hemingway in his 1926 novel, *The Sun Also Rises*, the definition of the Lost Generation applies to those born between 1883 and 1900 who came of age during World War I. The pioneering modernist work produced by authors during this period popularised an entirely new literary style and sensibility, championing the indulgent lifestyle the era became synonymous with.

As America moved away from its post-war sorrow, the country entered into a period of ecstasy and celebration. Technology was developing faster than ever, and America's economy rapidly expanded. The illegal trafficking of alcohol, known as bootlegging, was at its height, and speakeasies were immensely popular. As the economy grew, people became more frivolous and extravagant in spending. Cocktails and dances such as the Charleston were all the rage, and with the 19th Amendment granting women the right to vote, young people had newfound freedom. Jazz culture instigated a substantial societal shift. People of all races, genders, and backgrounds were mixing in underground bars. The decade gave way to new forms of self-expression and youth culture. It was the age of flapper girls, materialism, excessive drinking, and artistic genius.

The new social frivolity was captured in the decade's literature. Despite the term 'Jazz Age' being in existence before his writings, it was F. Scott Fitzgerald who popularised the phrase with the publication of his second collection of short stories, *Tales of the Jazz Age* (1922). One of the most influential writers of the Lost Generation, Fitzgerald's masterful works, including the now famous novel *The Great Gatsby* (1925), perfectly encapsulates the spirit of the time.

In the aftermath of the war, many members of the Lost Generation felt the US no longer had anything to offer them, so they took to travelling. Europe called to the artists who were seeking escape from the rising commercialism in the States, and it was in Paris that the likes of Hemingway and Fitzgerald first found their footing as authors, rubbing shoulders with the literary elite in the Parisian salons and cafés.

Often regarded as the mother of the Lost Generation writers, Gertrude Stein formed her own literary salon in Paris where poets, authors, musicians, and artists were able to seek guidance and counsel among peers. Similarly, Shakespeare and Company, an English-language lending library and bookstore in Paris, was also a haven for authors. American publisher Sylvia Beach opened the store in November 1919, with Stein signing up as her first annual subscriber. It's said that the store often served as a makeshift bedroom for Fitzgerald and Hemingway, amongst other writers.

Stein's memoir spoof, *The Autobiography of Alice B. Toklas* (1933), describes many of her encounters with the Lost Generation writers from the perspective of her life partner, Alice B. Toklas. The book is an account of the couple's time living in Paris during the Jazz Age, giving insight into the pair's relationship with these influential literary figures. From the likes of Sylvia Beach and Ezra Pound to T. S. Eliot and Carl Van Vechten, Stein and Toklas formed many literary friendships and connections in Paris, even becoming Godparents to Hemingway's first child.

While the era was a time of prosperity and hope, the war had caused long-lasting effects on the generations that followed. Young people were entering the 1920s with war wounds, both physical and emotional. Writers started to find escape within their art, creating written accounts of their experiences with the war becoming a common theme of Jazz Age literature. William Faulkner's first novel, *Soldiers' Pay* (1926), examines the reality of many returning soldiers. It explores the post-war life of a severely wounded aviator after he returns home and discovers he no longer has a purpose in his small town. Similar in its post-war themes, Hemingway's debut novel, *The Sun Also Rises* (1926), follows protagonist Jake Barnes as he navigates life after war. Based on Hemingway himself the main character is recovering from war wounds whilst working as a journalist in Paris. The early novel dismisses Stein's 'lost generation' label and proposes that they are not 'lost' but merely downtrodden by war. Exploring issues of artistic freedom, gender, love, and angst, *The Sun Also Rises* captures the essence of the disoriented generation.

Despite the existentialist questions that many of the Lost Generation writers addressed in their work, the Jazz Age also saw a significant shift in artists' sense of freedom. Writers were beginning to test the limits of literature, and modernist experimentation heightened. One of the most experimental writers of this time was e. e. cummings, whose work is rich in his war experiences. While serving as an ambulance driver in the war, cummings was arrested and imprisoned by the French on suspicion of espionage. This experience later informed the writing of his only novel, *The Enormous Room* (1922), which not only explores the psychological impact of war but also demonstrates his blossoming avant-garde writing style. The collections of poetry that followed, including *Tulips and Chimneys* (1923), *XLI Poems* (1925), & (1926), and *is 5* (1926), ignore traditional form and grammar rules, experiment with typographical presentation, and focus on taboo themes such as eroticism through an aggressive rebellion of accepted literary norms.

The Jazz Age not only gave the Lost Generation artistic freedom but also freedom of speech. Women now had the right to vote and could express themselves more independently. Through their newfound freedom, it became common for women to wear their hair short, dress in tight clothing, and smoke in public—a stereotype character consistently filling the pages of literature at the time. Anita Loos' comic novel *Gentlemen Prefer Blondes* (1925) is a prime example of this. The book features Lorelei Lee, a young blonde flapper, following her gold-digging escapades and numerous romantic flings around the world. Presented as Lorelei's diary, *Gentlemen Prefer Blondes* is full of Loos' famous wisecracks and takes the reader across the globe from New York and Paris to London and Munich, giving an insightful look at the Jazz Age on the way.

Another novel, *Firecrackers* (1925) by Carl Van Vechten, also encapsulates the sense of this newfound freedom. The book is known for its audacious events and pleasure-seeking characters, with Fitzgerald labelling one of its main characters, Campaspe Lorillard, as the 'embodiment of New York'. Likewise, Fitzgerald's own novel *The Great Gatsby* encompasses the excessive drinking and spending that was a crucial part of the Lost Generation's Jazz Age experience. Set on Long Island, New York, *Gatsby* features the confusing romance, corrupt morals, and glamorous partying of the city's most wealthy socialites. The effects of the prohibition and the popularity of jazz music are as evident in Vechten's work as they are in Fitzgerald's masterpiece.

Despite being labelled as 'lost', the young generation of the Jazz Age was hopeful and driven, transforming sorrow and grief into glittering inspiration for their work. Literature greatly benefited from writers' desire to escape, both in their travel to locations such as Paris and within their work. As the economy boomed, consumerism grew, and women slowly gained independence, artists captured the extravagance of the Roaring Twenties at its peak. The Jazz Age was an era of social reform that altered post-war America tremendously; it produced many brilliant authors whose written masterpieces shaped the foundation of literature as we now know it. From Gatsby to Hemingway, the Lost Generation writers of the American Jazz Age were driven by the lingering pain of the First World War to create works that are beautifully timeless. Embracing the chaos of post-war America to shape an era of cultural prosperity, one steeped in sparkling, glamorous indulgence.

GENTLEMEN
PREFER BLONDES

*"Kissing your hand may make you feel
very good but a diamond bracelet lasts forever."*

CHAPTER ONE

GENTLEMEN PREFER BLONDES

March 16th:

A gentleman friend and I were dining at the Ritz last evening and he said that if I took a pencil and a paper and put down all of my thoughts it would make a book. This almost made me smile as what it would really make would be a whole row of encyclopediacs. I mean I seem to be thinking practically all of the time. I mean it is my favorite recreation and sometimes I sit for hours and do not seem to do anything else but think. So this gentleman said a girl with brains ought to do something else with them besides think. And he said he ought to know brains when he sees them, because he is in the senate and he spends quite a great deal of time in Washington, d. c., and when he comes into contract with brains he always notices it. So it might have all blown over but this morning he sent me a book. And so when my maid brought it to me, I said to her, "Well, Lulu, here is another book and we have not read half the ones we have got yet." But when I opened it and saw that it was all a blank I remembered what my gentleman acquaintance said, and so then I realized that it was a diary. So here I am writing a book instead of reading one. But now it is the 16th of March and of course it is to late to begin with January, but it does not matter as my gentleman friend, Mr. Eisman, was in town practically all of January and February, and when he is in town one day seems to be practically the same as the next day.

I mean Mr. Eisman is in the wholesale button profession

in Chicago and he is the gentleman who is known practically all over Chicago as Gus Eisman the Button King. And he is the gentleman who is interested in educating me, so of course he is always coming down to New York to see how my brains have improved since the last time. But when Mr. Eisman is in New York we always seem to do the same thing and if I wrote down one day in my diary, all I would have to do would be to put quotation marks for all other days. I mean we always seem to have dinner at the Colony and see a show and go to the Trocadero and then Mr. Eisman shows me to my apartment. So of course when a gentleman is interested in educating a girl, he likes to stay and talk about the topics of the day until quite late, so I am quite fatigued the next day and I do not really get up until it is time to dress for dinner at the Colony.

It would be strange if I turn out to be an authoress. I mean at my home near Little Rock, Arkansas, my family all wanted me to do something about my music. Because all of my friends said I had talent and they all kept after me and kept after me about practising. But some way I never seemed to care so much about practising. I mean I simply could not sit for hours and hours at a time practising just for the sake of a career. So one day I got quite tempermental and threw the old mandolin clear across the room and I have really never touched it since. But writing is different because you do not have to learn or practise and it is more tempermental because practising seems to take all the temperment out of me. So now I really almost have to smile because I have just noticed that I have written clear across two pages onto March 18th, so this will do for today and tomorrow. And it just shows how tempermental I am when I get started.

"It would be strange if I turn out to be an authoress."

March 19th:

Well last evening Dorothy called up and Dorothy said she has met a gentleman who gave himself an introduction to her in the lobby of the Ritz. So then they went to luncheon and tea and dinner and then they went to a show and then they went to the Trocadero. So Dorothy said his name was Lord Cooksleigh but what she really calls him is Coocoo. So Dorothy said why don't you and I and Coocoo go to the Follies tonight and bring Gus along if he is in town? So then Dorothy and I had quite a little quarrel because every time that Dorothy mentions the subject of Mr. Eisman she calls Mr. Eisman by his first name, and she does not seem to realize that when a gentleman who is as important as Mr. Eisman, spends quite a lot of money educating a girl, it really does not show reverance to call a gentleman by his first name. I mean I never even think of calling Mr. Eisman by his first name, but if I want to call him anything at all, I call him "Daddy" and I do not even call him "Daddy" if a place seems to be public. So I told Dorothy that Mr. Eisman would not be in town until day after tomorrow. So then Dorothy and Coocoo came up and we went to the Follies.

So this morning Coocoo called up and he wanted me to luncheon at the Ritz. I mean these foreigners really have quite a nerve. Just because Coocoo is an Englishman and a Lord he thinks a girl can waste hours on him just for a luncheon at the Ritz, when all he does is talk about some exposition he went on to a place called Tibet and after talking for hours I found out that all they were was a lot of Chinamen. So I will be quite glad to see Mr. Eisman when he gets in. Because he always has something quite interesting to talk about, as for instants the last time he was here he presented me with quite a beautiful emerald bracelet. So next week is my birthday and he always has some delightful surprise on holidays.

I did intend to luncheon at the Ritz with Dorothy today and of course Coocoo had to spoil it, as I told him that I could not luncheon with him today, because my brother was in town on business and had the mumps, so I really could not leave him alone. Because of course if I went to the Ritz now I would bump into Coocoo. But I sometimes almost have to smile at my own imagination, because of course I have not got any brother and I have not even thought of the mumps for years. I mean it is no wonder that I can write.

So the reason I thought I would take luncheon at the Ritz was because Mr. Chaplin is at the Ritz and I always like to renew old acquaintances, because I met Mr. Chaplin once when we were both working on the same lot in Hollywood and I am sure he would remember me. Gentlemen always seem to remember blondes. I mean the only career I would like to be besides an authoress is a cinema star and I was doing quite well in the cinema when Mr. Eisman made me give it all up. Because of course when a gentleman takes such a friendly interest in educating a girl as Mr. Eisman does, you like to show that you appreciate it, and he is against a girl being in the cinema because his mother is authrodox.

March 20th:

Mr. Eisman gets in tomorrow to be here in time for my birthday. So I thought it would really be delightful to have at least one good time before Mr. Eisman got in, so last evening I had some literary gentlemen in to spend the evening because Mr. Eisman always likes me to have literary people in and out of the apartment. I mean he is quite anxious for a girl to improve her mind and his greatest interest in me is because I always seem to want to improve my mind and not waste any time. And Mr. Eisman likes me to have what the French people call a "salo" which means that people all get together in the evening and improve their minds. So I invited all of the brainy gentlemen I could think up. So I thought up a gentleman who is the proffessor of all of the economics up at Columbia College, and the editor who is the famous editor of the New York Transcript and another gentleman who is a famous playright who writes very, very famous plays that are all about Life. I mean anybody would recognize his name but it always seems to slip my memory because all of we real friends of his only call him Sam. So Sam asked if he could bring a gentleman who writes novels from England, so I said yes, so he brought him. And then we all got together and I called up Gloria and Dorothy and the gentleman brought their own liquor. So of course the place was a wreck this morning and Lulu and I worked like proverbial dogs to get it cleaned up, but Heaven knows how long it will take to get the chandelier fixed.

March 22nd:

Well my birthday has come and gone but it was really quite depressing. I mean it seems to me a gentleman who has a friendly interest in educating a girl like Gus Eisman, would want her to have the biggest square cut diamond in New York. I mean I must say I was quite disappointed when he came to the apartment with a little thing you could hardly see. So I told him I thought it was quite cute, but I had quite a headache and I had better stay in a dark room all day and I told him I would see him the next day, perhaps. Because even Lulu thought it was quite small and she said, if she was I, she really would do something definite and she said she always believed in the old addage, "Leave them while you're looking good." But he came in at dinner time with really a very very beautiful bracelet of square cut diamonds so I was quite cheered up. So then we had dinner at the Colony and we went to a show and supper at the Trocadero as usual whenever he is in town. But I will give him credit that he realized how small it was. I mean he kept talking about how bad business was and the button profession was full of bolshevicks who make nothing but trouble. Because Mr. Eisman feels that the country is really on the verge of the bolshevicks and I become quite worried. I mean if the bolshevicks do get in, there is only one gentleman who could handle them and that is Mr. D. W. Griffith. Because I will never forget when Mr. Griffith was directing Intolerance. I mean it was my last cinema just before Mr. Eisman made me give up my career and I was playing one of the girls that fainted at the battle when all of the gentlemen fell off the tower. And when I saw how Mr. Griffith handled all of those mobs in Intolerance I realized that he could do anything, and I really think that the government of America ought to tell Mr. Griffith to get all ready if the bolshevicks start to do it.

Well I forgot to mention that the English gentleman who writes novels seems to have taken quite an interest in me, as soon as he found out that I was literary. I mean he has called up every day and I went to tea twice with him. So he has sent me a whole complete set of books for my birthday by a gentleman called Mr. Conrad. They all seem to be about ocean travel although I have not had time to more than glance through them. I have always liked novels about ocean travel ever since I posed for Mr. Christie for the front cover of a novel about ocean travel by McGrath because I always say that a girl never really looks as well as she does on board a steamship, or even a yacht.

So the English gentleman's name is Mr. Gerald Lamson as those who have read his novels would know. And he also sent me some of his own novels and they all seem to be about middle age English gentlemen who live in the country over in London and seem to ride bicycles, which seems quite different from America, except at Palm Beach. So I told Mr. Lamson how I write down all of my thoughts and he said he knew I had something to me from the first minute he saw me and when we become better acquainted I am going to let him read my diary. I mean I even told Mr. Eisman about him and he is quite pleased. Because of course Mr. Lamson is quite famous and it seems Mr. Eisman has read all of his novels going to and fro on the trains and Mr. Eisman is always anxious to meet famous people and take them to the Ritz to dinner on Saturday night. But of course I did not tell Mr. Eisman that I am really getting quite a little crush on Mr. Lamson, which I really believe I am, but Mr. Eisman thinks my interest in him is more literary.

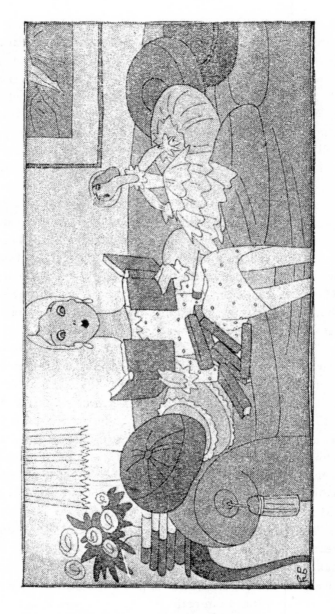

"He sent me a set of books by a gentleman called
Mr. Conrad. They all seem to be about ocean travel."

30

March 30th:

At last Mr. Eisman has left on the 20th Century and I must say I am quite fatigued and a little rest will be quite welcome. I mean I do not mind staying out late every night if I dance, but Mr. Eisman is really not such a good dancer so most of the time we just sit and drink some champagne or have a bite to eat and of course I do not dance with anyone else when I am out with Mr. Eisman. But Mr. Eisman and Gerry, as Mr. Lamson wants me to call him, became quite good friends and we had several evenings, all three together. So now that Mr. Eisman is out of town at last, Gerry and I are going out together this evening and Gerry said not to dress up, because Gerry seems to like me more for my soul. So I really had to tell Gerry that if all the gentlemen were like he seems to be, Madame Frances' whole dress making establishment would have to go out of business. But Gerry does not like a girl to be nothing else but a doll, but he likes her to bring in her husband's slippers every evening and make him forget what he has gone through.

But before Mr. Eisman went to Chicago he told me that he is going to Paris this summer on professional business and I think he intends to present me with a trip to Paris as he says there is nothing so educational as traveling. I mean it did worlds of good to Dorothy when she went abroad last spring and I never get tired of hearing her telling how the merry-go-rounds in Paris have pigs instead of horses. But I really do not know whether to be thrilled or not because, of course, if I go to Paris I will have to leave Gerry and both Gerry and I have made up our minds not to be separated from one another from now on.

March 31st:

Last night Gerry and I had dinner at quite a quaint place where we had roast beef and baked potato. I mean he always wants me to have food which is what he calls "nourishing" which most gentlemen never seem to think about.

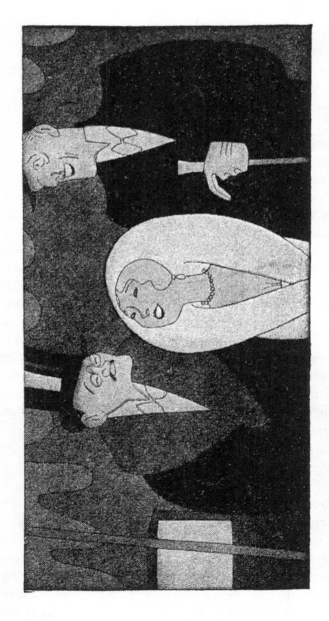

"I am really getting quite a little crush on Mr. Lamson
but Mr. Eisman thinks my interest in him is more literary."

So then we took a hansom cab and drove for hours around the park because Gerry said the air would be good for me. It is really very sweet to have some one think of all those things that gentlemen hardly ever seem to think about. So then we talked quite a lot. I mean Gerry knows how to draw a girl out and I told him things that I really would not even put in my diary. So when he heard all about my life he became quite depressed and we both had tears in our eyes. Because he said he never dreamed a girl could go through so much as I, and come out so sweet and not made bitter by it all. I mean Gerry thinks that most gentlemen are brutes and hardly ever think about a girl's soul.

So it seems that Gerry has had quite a lot of trouble himself and he can not even get married on account of his wife. He and she have never been in love with each other but she was a suffragette and asked him to marry her, so what could he do? So we rode all around the park until quite late talking and philosophizing quite a lot and I finally told him that I thought, after all, that bird life was the highest form of civilization. So Gerry calls me his little thinker and I really would not be surprised if all of my thoughts will give him quite a few ideas for his novels. Because Gerry says he has never seen a girl of my personal appearance with so many brains. And he had almost given up looking for his ideal when our paths seemed to cross each other and I told him I really thought a thing like that was nearly always the result of fate. So Gerry says that I remind him quite a lot of Helen of Troy, who was of Greek extraction. But the only Greek I know is a Greek gentleman by the name of Mr. Georgopolis who is really quite wealthy and he is what Dorothy and I call a "Shopper" because you can always call him up at any hour and ask him to go shopping and he is always quite delighted, which very few gentlemen seem to be. And he never seems to care how much anything costs. I mean Mr. Georgopolis is also quite cultured, as I know quite a few gentlemen who can speak to a waiter in French but Mr. Georgopolis can also speak to a waiter in Greek which very few gentlemen seem to be able to do.

April 1st:

I am taking special pains with my diary from now on as I am really writing it for Gerry. I mean he and I are going to read it together some evening in front of the fireplace. But Gerry leaves this evening for Boston as he has to lecture about all of his works at Boston, but he will rush right back as soon as possible. So I am going to spend all of my time improving myself while he is gone. And this afternoon we are both going to a museum on 5th Avenue, because Gerry wants to show me a very very beautiful cup made by an antique jeweler called Mr. Cellini and he wants me to read Mr. Cellini's life which is a very very fine book and not dull while he is in Boston.

So the famous playright friend of mine who is called Sam called up this morning and he wanted me to go to a literary party tonight that he and some other literary gentlemen are giving to Florence Mills in Harlem but Gerry does not want me to go with Sam as Sam always insists on telling riskay stories. But personally I am quite broad minded and I always say that I do not mind a riskay story as long as it is really funny. I mean I have a great sense of humor. But Gerry says Sam does not always select and choose his stories and he just as soon I did not go out with him. So I am going to stay home and read the book by Mr. Cellini instead, because, after all, the only thing I am really interested in, is improving my mind. So I am going to do nothing else but improve my mind while Gerry is in Boston. I mean I just received a cable from Willie Gwynn who arrives from Europe tomorrow, but I am not even going to bother to see him. He is a sweet boy but he never gets anywhere and I am not going to waste my time on such as him, after meeting a gentleman like Gerry.

April 2nd:

I seem to be quite depressed this morning as I always am when there is nothing to put my mind to. Because I decided not to read the book by Mr. Cellini. I mean it was quite amuseing in spots because it was really quite riskay but the spots were not so close together and I never seem to like to always be hunting clear through a book for the spots I am looking for, especially when there are really not so many spots that seem to be so amuseing after all. So I did not waste my time on it but this morning I told Lulu to let all of the house work go and spend the day reading a book entitled "Lord Jim" and then tell me all about it, so that I would improve my mind while Gerry is away. But when I got her the book I nearly made a mistake and gave her a book by the title of "The Nigger of the Narcissus" which really would have hurt her feelings. I mean I do not know why authors cannot say "Negro" instead of "Nigger" as they have their feelings just the same as we have.

Well I just got a telegram from Gerry that he will not be back until tomorrow and also some orchids from Willie Gwynn, so I may as well go to the theatre with Willie tonight to keep from getting depressed, as he really is a sweet boy after all. I mean he never really does anything obnoxious. And it is quite depressing to stay at home and do nothing but read, unless you really have a book that is worth bothering about.

April 3rd:

I was really so depressed this morning that I was even glad to get a letter from Mr. Eisman. Because last night Willie Gwynn came to take me to the Follies, but he was so intoxicated that I had to telephone his club to send around a taxi to take him home. So that left me alone with Lulu at nine o'clock with nothing to do, so I put in a telephone call for Boston to talk to Gerry but it never went through. So Lulu tried to teach me how to play mah jong, but I really could not keep my mind on it because I was so depressed. So today I think I had better go over to Madame Frances and order some new evening gowns to cheer me up.

Well Lulu just brought me a telegram from Gerry that he will be in this afternoon, but I must not meet him at the station on account of all of the reporters who always meet him at the station wherever he comes from. But he says he will come right up to see me as he has something to talk about.

April 4th:

What an evening we had last evening. I mean it seems that Gerry is madly in love with me. Because all of the time he was in Boston lecturing to the womens clubs he said, as he looked over the faces of all those club women in Boston, he never realized I was so beautiful. And he said that there was only one in all the world and that was me. But it seems that Gerry thinks that Mr. Eisman is terrible and that no good can come of our friendship. I mean I was quite surprised, as they both seemed to get along quite well together, but it seems that Gerry never wants me to see Mr. Eisman again. And he wants me to give up everything and study French and he will get a divorce and we will be married. Because Gerry does not seem to like the kind of life all of us lead in New York and he wants me to go home to papa in Arkansas and he will send me books to read so that I will not get lonesome there. And he gave me his uncle's Masonic ring, which came down from the time of Soloman and which he never even lets his wife wear, for our engagement ring, and this afternoon a lady friend of his is going to bring me a new system she thought up of how to learn French. But some way I still seem to be depressed. I mean I could not sleep all night thinking of the terrible things Gerry said about New York and about Mr. Eisman. Of course I can understand Gerry being jealous of any gentleman friend of mine and of course I never really thought that Mr. Eisman was Rudolph Valentino, but Gerry said it made him cringe to think of a sweet girl like I having a friendship with Mr. Eisman. So it really made me feel quite depressed. I mean Gerry likes to talk quite a lot and I always think a lot of talk is depressing and worries your brains with things you never even think of when you are busy.

*"He said it made him cringe to think of a
sweet girl like I having a friendship with Mr. Eisman."*

But so long as Gerry does not mind me going out with other gentlemen when they have something to give you mentally, I am going to luncheon with Eddie Goldmark of the Goldmark Films who is always wanting me to sign a contract to go into the cinema. Because Mr. Goldmark is madly in love with Dorothy and Dorothy is always wanting me to go back in the cinema because Dorothy says that she will go if I will go.

April 6th:

Well I finally wrote Mr. Eisman that I was going to get married and it seems that he is coming on at once as he would probably like to give me his advice. Getting married is really quite serious and Gerry talks to me for hours and hours about it. I mean he never seems to get tired of talking and he does not seem to even want to go to shows or dance or do anything else but talk, and if I don't really have something definite to put my mind on soon I will scream.

April 7th:

Well Mr. Eisman arrived this morning and he and I had quite a long talk, and after all I think he is right. Because here is the first real opportunity I have ever really had. I mean to go to Paris and broaden out and improve my writing, and why should I give it up to marry an author, where he is the whole thing and all I would be would be the wife of Gerald Lamson? And on top of that I would have to be dragged into the scandal of a divorce court and get my name smirched. So Mr. Eisman said that opportunities come to seldom in a girls life for me to give up the first one I have really ever had. So I am sailing for France and London on Tuesday and taking Dorothy with me and Mr. Eisman says that he will see us there later. So Dorothy knows all of the ropes and she can get along in Paris just as though she knew French and besides she knows a French gentleman who was born and raised there, who speaks it like a native and knows Paris like a book.

"He said I would be dragged into the scandal
of a divorce court and get my name smirched."

And Dorothy says that when we get to London nearly everybody speaks English anyway. So it is quite lucky that Mr. Lamson is out lecturing in Cincinnati and he will not be back until Wednesday and I can send him a letter and tell him that I have to go to Europe now but I will see him later perhaps. So anyway I will be spared listening to any more of his depressing conversation. So Mr. Eisman gave me quite a nice string of pearls and he gave Dorothy a diamond pin and we all went to the Colony for dinner and we all went to a show and supper at the Trocadero and we all spent quite a pleasant evening.

*"So I am sailing for France and London on Tuesday and
taking Dorothy with me and Mr. Eisman will see us there later."*

41

CHAPTER TWO

FATE KEEPS ON HAPPENING

April 11th:

Well Dorothy and I are really on the ship sailing to Europe as anyone could tell by looking at the ocean. I always love the ocean. I mean I always love a ship and I really love the *Majestic* because you would not know it was a ship because it is just like being at the Ritz, and the steward says the ocean is not so obnoxious this month as it generally is. So Mr. Eisman is going to meet us next month in Paris because he has to be there on business. I mean he always says that there is really no place to see the latest styles in buttons like Paris.

So Dorothy is out taking a walk up and down the deck with a gentleman she met on the steps, but I am not going to waste my time going around with gentlemen because if I did nothing but go around I would not finish my diary or read good books which I am always reading to improve my mind. But Dorothy really does not care about her mind and I always scold her because she does nothing but waste her time by going around with gentlemen who do not have anything, when Eddie Goldmark of the Goldmark Films is really quite wealthy and can make a girl delightful presents. But she does nothing but waste her time and yesterday, which was really the day before we sailed, she would not go to luncheon with Mr. Goldmark but she went to luncheon to meet a gentleman called Mr. Mencken from Baltimore who really only prints a green magazine which has not even got any pictures in it. But Mr. Eisman is always saying that every girl

43

does not want to get ahead and get educated like me.

So Mr. Eisman and Lulu come down to the boat to see me off and Lulu cried quite a lot. I mean I really believe she could not care any more for me if she was light and not colored. Lulu has had a very sad life because when she was quite young a pullman porter fell madly in love with her. So she believed him and he lured her away from her home to Ashtabula and deceived her there. So she finally found out that she had been deceived and she really was broken hearted and when she tried to go back home she found out that it was to late because her best girl friend, who she had always trusted, had stolen her husband and he would not take Lulu back. So I have always said to her she could always work for me and she is going to take care of the apartment until I get back, because I would not sublet the apartment because Dorothy sublet her apartment when she went to Europe last year and the gentleman who sublet the apartment allowed girls to pay calls on him who were not nice.

Mr. Eisman has litereally filled our room with flowers and the steward has had quite a hard time to find enough vases to put them into. I mean the steward said he knew as soon as he saw Dorothy and I that he would have quite a heavy run on vases. And of course Mr. Eisman has sent me quite a lot of good books as he always does, because he always knows that good books are always welcome. So he has sent me quite a large book of Etiquette as he says there is quite a lot of Etiquette in England and London and it would be a good thing for a girl to learn. So I am going to take it on the deck after luncheon and read it, because I would often like to know what a girl ought to do when a gentleman she has just met, says something to her in a taxi. Of course I always become quite vexed but I always believe in giving a gentleman another chance. So now the steward tells me it is luncheon time, so I will go upstairs as the gentleman Dorothy met on the steps has invited us to luncheon in the Ritz, which is a special dining room on the ship where you can spend quite a lot of money because they really give away the food in the other dining room.

*"The steward said he knew as soon as he saw Dorothy
and I that he would have quite a heavy run on vases."*

April 12th:

I am going to stay in bed this morning as I am quite upset as I saw a gentleman who quite upset me. I am not really sure it was the gentleman, as I saw him at quite a distants in the bar, but if it really is the gentleman it shows that when a girl has a lot of fate in her life it is sure to keep on happening. So when I thought I saw this gentleman I was with Dorothy and Major Falcon, who is the gentleman Dorothy met on the steps, and Major Falcon noticed that I became upset, so he wanted me to tell him what was the matter, but it is really so terrible that I would not want to tell anyone. So I said good night to Major Falcon and I left him with Dorothy and I went down to our room and did nothing but cry and send the steward for some champagne to cheer me up. I mean champagne always makes me feel philosophical because it makes me realize that when a girl's life is as full of fate as mine seems to be, there is nothing else to do about it. So this morning the steward brought me my coffee and quite a large pitcher of ice water so I will stay in bed and not have any more champagne until luncheon time.

Dorothy never has any fate in her life and she does nothing but waste her time and I really wonder if I did right to bring her with me and not Lulu. I mean she really gives gentlemen a bad impression as she talks quite a lot of slang. Because when I went up yesterday to meet she and Major Falcon for luncheon, I overheard her say to Major Falcon that she really liked to become intoxicated once in a "dirty" while. Only she did not say intoxicated, but she really said a slang word that means intoxicated and I am always having to tell her that "dirty" is a slang word and she really should not say "dirty."

Major Falcon is really quite a delightful gentleman for an Englishman. I mean he really spends quite a lot of money and we had quite a delightful luncheon and dinner in the Ritz until I thought I saw the gentleman who upset me and I am so upset I think I will get dressed and go up on the deck and see if it really is the one I think it is.

*"I overheard Dorothy tell Major Falcon that
she liked to become intoxicated once in a dirty while."*

I mean there is nothing else for me to do as I have finished writing in my diary for today and I have decided not to read the book of Ettiquette as I glanced through it and it does not seem to have anything in it that I would care to know because it wastes quite a lot of time telling you what to call a Lord and all the Lords I have met have told me what to call them and it is generally some quite cute name like Coocoo whose real name is really Lord Cooksleigh. So I will not waste my time on such a book. But I wish I did not feel so upset about the gentleman I think I saw.

April 13th:
It really is the gentleman I thought I saw. I mean when I found out it was the gentleman my heart really stopped. Because it all brought back things that anybody does not like to remember, no matter who they are. So yesterday when I went up on the deck to see if I could see the gentleman and see if it really was him, I met quite a delightful gentleman who I met once at a party called Mr. Ginzberg. Only his name is not Mr. Ginzberg any more because a gentleman in London called Mr. Battenburg, who is some relation to some king, changed his name to Mr. Mountbatten which Mr. Ginzberg says really means the same thing after all. So Mr. Ginsberg changed his name to Mr. Mountginz which he really thinks is more aristocratic. So we walked around the deck and we met the gentleman face to face and I really saw it was him and he really saw it was me. I mean his face became so red it was almost a picture. So I was so upset I said good-bye to Mr. Mountginz and I started to rush right down to my room and cry. But when I was going down the steps, I bumped right into Major Falcon who noticed that I was upset. So Major Falcon made me go to the Ritz and have some champagne and tell him all about it.

So then I told Major Falcon about the time in Arkansas when Papa sent me to Little Rock to study how to become a stenographer.

*"So Mr. Ginsberg changed his name to
Mr. Mountginz which he really thinks is more aristocratic."*

I mean Papa and I had quite a little quarrel because Papa did not like a gentleman who used to pay calls on me in the park and Papa thought it would do me good to get away for awhile. So I was in the business colledge in Little Rock for about a week when a gentleman called Mr. Jennings paid a call on the business colledge because he wanted to have a new stenographer. So he looked over all we colledge girls and he picked me out. So he told our teacher that he would help me finish my course in his office because he was only a lawyer and I really did not have to know so much. So Mr. Jennings helped me quite a lot and I stayed in his office about a year when I found out that he was not the kind of a gentleman that a young girl is safe with. I mean one evening when I went to pay a call on him at his apartment, I found a girl there who really was famous all over Little Rock for not being nice. So when I found out that girls like that paid calls on Mr. Jennings I had quite a bad case of histerics and my mind was really a blank and when I came out of it, it seems that I had a revolver in my hand and it seems that the revolver had shot Mr. Jennings.

So this gentleman on the boat was really the District Attorney who was at the trial and he really was quite harsh at the trial and he called me names that I would not even put in my diary. Because everyone at the trial except the District Attorney was really lovely to me and all the gentlemen in the jury all cried when my lawyer pointed at me and told them that they practically all had had either a mother or a sister. So the jury was only out three minutes and then they came back and acquitted me and they were all so lovely that I really had to kiss all of them and when I kissed the judge he had tears in his eyes and he took me right home to his sister. I mean it was when Mr. Jennings became shot that I got the idea to go into the cinema, so Judge Hibbard got me a ticket to Hollywood. So it was Judge Hibbard who really gave me my name because he did not like the name I had because he said a girl ought to have a name that ought to express her personality.

*"So when they acquitted me I kissed
the judge and they all had tears in their eyes."*

So he said my name ought to be Lorelei which is the name of a girl who became famous for sitting on a rock in Germany, So I was in Hollywood in the cinema when I met Mr. Eisman and he said that a girl with my brains ought not to be in the cinema but she ought to be educated, so he took me out of the cinema so he could educate me.

So Major Falcon was really quite interested in everything I talked about, because he said it was quite a co-instance because this District Attorney, who is called Mr. Bartlett, is now working for the government of America and he is on his way to a place called Vienna on some business for Uncle Sam that is quite a great secret and Mr. Falcon would like very much to know what the secret is, because the Government in London sent him to America especially to find out what it was. Only of course Mr. Bartlett does not know who Major Falcon is, because it is such a great secret, but Major Falcon can tell me, because he knows who he can trust. So Major Falcon says he thinks a girl like I ought to forgive and forget what Mr. Bartlett called me and he wants to bring us together and he says he thinks Mr. Bartlett would talk to me quite a lot when he really gets to know me and I forgive him for that time in Little Rock. Because it would be quite romantic for Mr. Bartlett and I to become friendly, and gentlemen who work for Uncle Sam generally like to become romantic with girls. So he is going to bring us together on the deck after dinner tonight and I am going to forgive him and talk with him quite a lot, because why should a girl hold a grudge against a gentleman who had to do it. So Major Falcon brought me quite a large bottle of perfume and a quite cute imitation of quite a large size dog in the little shop which is on board the boat. I mean Major Falcon really knows how to cheer a girl up quite a lot and so tonight I am going to make it all up with Mr. Bartlett.

April 14th:

Well Mr. Bartlett and I made it all up last night and we are going to be the best of friends and talk quite a lot. So when I went down to my room quite late Major Falcon came down to see if I and Mr. Bartlett were really going to be friends because he said a girl with brains like I ought to have lots to talk about with a gentleman with brains like Mr. Bartlett who knows all of Uncle Sam's secrets.

So I told Major Falcon how Mr. Bartlett thinks that he and I seem to be like a play, because all the time he was calling me all those names in Little Rock he really thought I was. So when he found out that I turned out not to be, he said he always thought that I only used my brains against gentlemen and really had quite a cold heart. But now he thinks I ought to write a play about how he called me all those names in Little Rock and then, after seven years, we became friendly.

So I told Major Falcon that I told Mr. Bartlett I would like to write the play but I really did not have time as it takes quite a lot of time to write my diary and read good books. So Mr. Bartlett did not know that I read books which is quite a co-instance because he reads them to. So he is going to bring me a book of philosophy this afternoon called "Smile, Smile, Smile" which all the brainy senators in Washington are reading which cheers you up quite a lot.

So I told Major Falcon that having a friendship with Mr. Barlett was really quite enervating because Mr. Bartlett does not drink anything and the less anybody says about his dancing the better. But he did ask me to dine at his table, which is not in the Ritz and I told him I could not, but Major Falcon told me I ought to, but I told Major Falcon that there was a limit to almost everything. So I am going to stay in my room until luncheon and I am going to luncheon in the Ritz with Mr. Mountginz who really knows how to treat a girl.

*"The steward has had quite a sad life
and he likes to tell me all about himself."*

Dorothy is up on the deck wasting quite a lot of time with a gentleman who is only a tennis champion. So I am going to ring for the steward and have some champagne which is quite good for a person on a boat. The steward is really quite a nice boy and he has had quite a sad life and he likes to tell me all about himself. I mean it seems that he was arrested in Flatbush because he promised a gentleman that he would bring him some very very good scotch and they mistook him for a bootlegger. So it seems they put him in a prison and they put him in a cell with two other gentlemen who were very, very famous burglars. I mean they really had their pictures in all the newspapers and everybody was talking about them. So my steward, whose real name is Fred, was very very proud to be in the same cell with such famous burglars. So when they asked him what he was in for, he did not like to tell them that he was only a bootlegger, so he told them that he set fire to a house and burned up quite a large family in Oklahoma. So everything would have gone alright except that the police had put a dictaphone in the cell and used it all against him and he could not get out until they had investigated all the fires in Oklahoma. So I always think that it is much more educational to talk to a boy like Fred who has been through a lot and really suffered than it is to talk to a gentleman like Mr. Bartlett. But I will have to talk to Mr. Bartlett all afternoon as Major Falcon has made an appointment for me to spend the whole afternoon with him.

April 15th:

Last night there was quite a maskerade ball on the ship which was really all for the sake of charity because most of the sailors seem to have orphans which they get from going on the ocean when the sea is very rough. So they took up quite a collection and Mr. Bartlett made quite a long speech in favor of orphans especially when their parents are sailors. Mr. Bartlett really likes to make speeches quite a lot. I mean he even likes to make speeches when he is all alone with a girl when they are walking up and down a deck. But the maskerade ball was quite cute and one gentleman really looked almost like an imitation of Mr. Chaplin. So Dorothy and I really did not want to go to the ball but Mr. Bartlett bought us two scarfs at the little store which is on the ship so we tied them around our hips and everyone said we made quite a cute Carmen. So Mr. Bartlett and Major Falcon and the tennis champion were the Judges. So Dorothy and I won the prizes. I mean I really hope I do not get any more large size imitations of a dog as I have three now and I do not see why the Captain does not ask Mr. Cartier to have a jewelry store on the ship as it is really not much fun to go shopping on a ship with gentlemen, and buy nothing but imitations of dogs.

So after we won the prizes I had an engagement to go up on the top of the deck with Mr. Bartlett as it seems he likes to look at the moonlight quite a lot. So I told him to go up and wait for me and I would be up later as I promised a dance to Mr. Mountginz. So he asked me how long I would be dancing till, but I told him to wait up there and he would find out. So Mr. Mountginz and I had quite a delightful dance and champagne until Major Falcon found us. Because he was looking for me and he said I really should not keep Mr. Bartlett waiting. So I went up on the deck and Mr. Bartlett was up there waiting for me and it seems that he really is madly in love with me because he did not sleep a wink since we became friendly. Because he never thought that I really had brains but now that he knows it, it seems that he has been looking for a girl like me for years, and he said that really the place for me when he got back home was Washington d. c. where he lives. So I told him I thought a thing like that was nearly always the result of fate. So he wanted me to get off the ship tomorrow at France and take the same trip that he is taking to Vienna as it seems that Vienna is in France and if you go on to England you go to far. But I told him that I could not because I thought that if he was really madly in love with me he would take a trip to London instead.

*"Mr. Bartlett said he did not
sleep a wink since we became friendly."*

But he told me that he had serious business in Vienna that was a very, very great secret. But I told him I did not believe it was business but that it really was some girl, because what business could be so important? So he said it was business for the United States government at Washington and he could not tell anybody what it was. So then we looked at the moonlight quite a lot. So I told him I would go to Vienna if I really knew it was business and not some girl, because I could not see how business could be so important. So then he told me all about it. So it seems that Uncle Sam wants some new aeroplanes that everybody else seems to want, especially England, and Uncle Sam has quite a clever way to get them which is to long to put in my diary. So we sat up and saw the sun rise and I became quite stiff and told him I would have to go down to my room because, after all, the ship lands at France today and I said if I got off the boat at France to go to Vienna with him I would have to pack up.

So I went down to my room and went to bed. So then Dorothy came in and she was up on the deck with the tennis champion but she did not notice the sun rise as she really does not love nature but always wastes her time and ruins her clothes even though I always tell her not to drink champagne out of a bottle on the deck of the ship as it lurches quite a lot. So I am going to have luncheon in my room and I will send a note to Mr. Bartlett to tell him I will not be able to get off the boat at France to go to Vienna with him as I have quite a headache, but I will see him sometime somewhere else. So Major Falcon is going to come down at 12 and I have got to thinking over what Mr. Bartlett called me at Little Rock and I am quite upset. I mean a gentleman never pays for those things but a girl always pays. So I think I will tell Major Falcon all about the airoplane business as he really wants to know. And, after all I do not think Mr. Bartlett is a gentleman to call me all those names in Little Rock even if it was seven years ago. I mean Major Falcon is always a gentleman and he really wants to do quite a lot for us in London. Because he knows the Prince of Wales and he thinks that Dorothy and

I would like the Prince of Wales once we had really got to meet him. So I am going to stay in my room until Mr. Bartlett gets off the ship at France, because I really do not seem to care if I never see Mr. Bartlett again.

So tomorrow we will be at England bright and early. And I really feel quite thrilled because Mr. Eisman sent me a cable this morning, as he does every morning, and he says to take advantage of everybody we meet as traveling is the highest form of education. I mean Mr. Eisman is always right and Major Falcon knows all the sights in London including the Prince of Wales so it really looks like Dorothy and I would have quite a delightful time in London.

CHAPTER THREE

LONDON IS REALLY NOTHING

April 17th:

Well, Dorothy and I are really at London. I mean we got to London on the train yesterday as the boat does not come clear up to London but it stops on the beach and you have to take a train. I mean everything is much better in New York, because the boat comes right up to New York and I am really beginning to think that London is not so educational after all. But I did not tell Mr. Eisman when I cabled him last night because Mr. Eisman really sent me to London to get educated and I would hate to tell him that London is a failure because we know more in New York.

So Dorothy and I came to the Ritz and it is delightfully full of Americans. I mean you would really think it was New York because I always think that the most delightful thing about traveling is to always be running into Americans and to always feel at home.

So yesterday Dorothy and I went down to luncheon at the Ritz and we saw a quite cute little blond girl at the next table and I nudged Dorothy under the table, because I do not think it is nice to nudge a person on top of the table as I am trying to teach good manners to Dorothy. So I said "That is quite a cute little girl so she must be an American girl." And sure enough she called the head-waiter with quite an American accent and she was quite angry and she said to him, I have been coming to this hotel for 35 years and this is the first time I have been kept waiting. So I recognized her voice because it was really Fanny Ward. So we asked her to come over to our table and we were all three delighted to see each other. Because I and Fanny have known each other for about five years but I really feel as if I knew her better because mama knew her 45 years ago when she and mama used to go to school together and mama used to always follow all her weddings in all the newspapers. So now Fanny lives in London and is famous for being one of the cutest girls in London. I mean Fanny is almost historical, because when a girl is cute for 50 years it really begins to get historical.

So if mama did not die of hardening of the arterys she and Fanny and I could have quite a delightful time in London as Fanny loves to shop. So we went shopping for hats and instead of going to the regular shop we went to the childrens department and Fanny and I bought some quite cute hats as childrens hats only cost half as much and Fanny does it all the time. I mean Fanny really loves hats and she buys some in the children's department every week, so she really saves quite a lot of money.

So we came back to the Ritz to meet Major Falcon because Major Falcon invited us to go to tea with him at a girls house called Lady Shelton. So Major Falcon invited Fanny to go with us to, but she was sorry because she had to go to her music lesson.

So at Lady Sheltons house we met quite a few people who seemed to be English. I mean some of the girls in London seem to be Ladies which seems to be the opposite of a Lord. And some who are not Ladies are honorable. But quite a few are not Ladies or honorable either, but are just like us, so all you have to call them is "Miss." So Lady Shelton was really delighted to have we Americans come to her house. I mean she took Dorothy and I into the back parlor and tried to sell us some shell flowers she seems to make out of sea shells for 25 pounds. So we asked her how much it was in money and it seems it is 125 dollars. I mean I am really going to have a quite hard time in London with Dorothy because she really should not say to an English lady what she said.

"So I recognized her voice because it was really Fanny Ward."

I mean she should not say to an English lady that in America we use shells the same way only we put a dry pea under one of them and we call it a game. But I told Lady Shelton we really did not need any shell flowers. So Lady Shelton said she knew we Americans loved dogs so she would love us to meet her mother.

So then she took Dorothy and Major Falcon and I to her mother's house which was just around the corner from her house. Because her mother seems to be called a Countess and raise dogs. So her mother was having a party too, and she seemed to have quite red hair and quite a lot of paint for such an elderly lady. So the first thing she asked us was she asked us if we bought some shell flowers from her daughter. So we told her no. But she did not seem to act like a Countess of her elderly age should act. Because she said, "You were right my dears—don't let my daughter stick you—they fall apart in less than a week." So then she asked us if we would like to buy a dog. I mean I could not stop Dorothy but she said "How long before the dogs fall apart?" But I do not think the Countess acted like a Countess ought to act because she laughed very, very loud and she said that Dorothy was really priceless and she grabbed Dorothy and kissed her and held her arm around her all the time. I mean I really think that a Countess should not encouradge Dorothy or else she is just as unrefined as Dorothy seems to be. But I told the Countess that we did not need any dog.

So then I met quite a delightful English lady who had a very, very beautiful diamond tiara in her hand bag because she said that she thought some Americans would be at the party and it was really a very, very great bargain. I mean I think a diamond tiara is delightful because it is a place where I really never thought of wearing diamonds before, and I thought I had almost one of everything until I saw a diamond tiara. The English lady who is called Mrs. Weeks said it was in her family for years but the good thing about diamonds is they always look new. So I was really very intreeged and I asked her how much it cost in money and it seems it was $7,500.

*"I told Sir Francis Beekman that
I really thought it looked quite cute."*

So then I looked around the room and I noticed a gentleman who seemed to be quite well groomed. So I asked Major Falcon who he was and he said he was called Sir Francis Beekman and it seems he is very, very wealthy. So then I asked Major Falcon to give us an introduction to one another and we met one another and I asked Sir Francis Beekman if he would hold my hat while I could try on the diamond tiara because I could wear it backwards with a ribbon, on account of my hair being hobbed, and I told Sir Francis Beekman that I really thought it looked quite cute. So he thought it did to, but he seemed to have another engagement. So the Countess came up to me and she is really very unrefined because she said to me "Do not waste your time on him" because she said that whenever Sir Francis Beekman spent a haypenny the statue of a gentleman called Mr. Nelson took off his hat and bowed. I mean some people are so unrefined they seem to have unrefined thoughts about everything.

So I really have my heart set on the diamond tiara and I became quite worried because Mrs. Weeks said she was going to a delightful party last night that would be full of delightful Americans and it would be snaped up. So I was so worried that I gave her 100 dollars and she is going to hold the diamond tiara for me. Because what is the use of traveling if you do not take advantadge of oportunities and it really is quite unusual to get a bargain from an English lady. So last night I cabled Mr. Eisman and I told Mr. Eisman that he does not seem to how know much it costs to get educated by traveling and I said I really would have to have $10,000 and I said I hoped I would not have to borrow the money from some strange English gentleman, even if he might be very very good looking. So I really could not sleep all night because of all of my worrying because if I do not get the money to buy the diamond tiara it may be a quite hard thing to get back $100 from an English lady. So now I must really get dressed as Major Falcon is going to take Dorothy and I to look at all the sights in London. But I really think if I do not get the diamond tiara my whole trip to London will be quite a failure.

April 18th:
Yesterday was quite a day and night. I mean Major Falcon came to take Dorothy and I to see all the sights in London. So I thought it would be delightful if we had another gentleman and I made Major Falcon call up Sir Francis Beekman. I mean I had a cable from Mr. Eisman which told me he could not send me 10,000 dollars but he would send me 1000 dollars which really would not be a drop in the bucket for the diamond tiara. So Sir Francis Beekman said that he could not come but I teased him and teased him over the telephone so he finally said he would come.

So Major Falcon drives his own car so Dorothy sat with him and I sat with Sir Francis Beekman but I told him that I was not going to call him Sir Francis Beekman but I was really going to call him Piggie.

In London they make a very, very great fuss over nothing at all. I mean London is really nothing at all. For instants, they make a great fuss over a tower that really is not even as tall as the Hickox building in Little Rock Arkansas and it would only make a chimney on one of our towers in New York. So Sir Francis Beekman wanted us to get out and look at the tower because he said that quite a famous Queen had her head cut off there one morning and Dorothy said "What a fool she was to get up that morning" and that is really the only sensible thing that Dorothy has said in London. So we did not bother to get out.

So we did not go to any more sights because they really have delicious champagne cocktails at a very very smart new restaurant called the Cafe de Paris that you could not get in New York for neither love or money and I told Piggie that when you are travelling you really ought to take advantadges of what you can not do at home.

So while Dorothy and I were in the Cafe de Paris powdering our nose in the lady's dressing room we met an American girl who Dorothy knew in the Follies, but now she is living in London.

*"In London they make a fuss over a tower that
is not as tall as the Hickox Building in Little Rock."*

So she told us all about London. So it seems the gentlemen in London have quite a quaint custom of not giving a girl many presents. I mean the English girls really seem to be satisfied with a gold cigaret holder or else what they call a 'bangle' which means a bracelet in English which is only gold and does not have any stones in it which American girls would really give to their maid. So she said you could tell what English gentlemen were like when you realize that not even English ladys could get anything out of them. So she said Sir Francis Beekman was really famous all over London for not spending so much money as most English gentlemen. So then Dorothy and I said goodbye to Dorothy's girl friend and Dorothy said, "Lets tell our two boy friends that we have a headache and go back to the Ritz, where men are Americans." Because Dorothy said that the society of a gentleman like Sir Francis Beekman was to great a price to pay for a couple of rounds of champagne cocktails. But I told Dorothy that I always believe that there is nothing like trying and I think it would be nice for an American girl like I to educate an English gentleman like Piggie, as I call Sir Francis Beekman.

So then we went back to the table and I almost have to admit that Dorothy is in the right about Piggie because he really likes to talk quite a lot and he is always talking about a friend of his who was quite a famous King in London called King Edward. So Piggie said he would never never forget the jokes King Edward was always saying and he would never forget one time they were all on a yacht and they were all sitting at a table and King Edward got up and said "I don't care what you gentlemen do—I'm going to smoke a cigar." So then Piggie laughed very, very loud. So of course I laughed very, very loud and I told Piggie he was wonderful the way he could tell jokes. I mean you can always tell when to laugh because Piggie always laughs first.

So in the afternoon a lot of lady friends of Mrs. Weeks heard about me buying the diamond tiara and called us up and asked us to their house to tea so Dorothy and I went and we took a gentleman Dorothy met in the lobby who is very, very good looking but he is only an English ballroom dancer in a cafe when he has a job.

So we went to tea to a lady's house called Lady Elmsworth and what she has to sell we Americans seems to be a picture of her father painted in oil paint who she said was a whistler. But I told her my own father was a whistler and used to whistle all of the time and I did not even have a picture of him but every time he used to go to Little Rock I asked him to go to the photographers but he did not go.

So then we met a lady called Lady Chizzleby that wanted us to go to her house to tea but we told her that we really did not want to buy anything. But she said that she did not have anything to sell but she wanted to borrow five pounds. So we did not go and I am really glad that Mr. Eisman did not come to London as all the English ladys would ask him to tea and he would have a whole ship load of shell flowers and dogs and anteek pictures that do nobody any good.

So last night Piggie and I and Dorothy and the dancer who is called Gerald went to the Kit Kat Club as Gerald had nothing better to do because he is out of a job. So Dorothy and I had quite a little quarrel because I told Dorothy that she was wasting quite a lot of time going with any gentleman who is out of a job but Dorothy is always getting to really like somebody and she will never learn how to act. I mean I always seem to think that when a girl really enjoys being with a gentleman, it puts her to quite a disadvantage and no real good can come of it.

Well tonight is going to be quite a night because Major Falcon is going to take Dorothy and I to a dance at a lady's house tonight to meet the Prince of Wales. And now I must get ready to see Piggie because he and I seem to be getting to be quite good friends even if he has not sent me any flowers yet.

April 19th:
Last night we really met the Prince of Wales. I mean Major Falcon called for Dorothy and I at eleven and took us to a ladys

house where the lady was having a party. The Prince of Wales is really wonderful. I mean even if he was not a prince he would be wonderful, because even if he was not a prince, he would be able to make his living playing the ukelele, if he had a little more practice. So the lady came up to me and told me that the Prince of Wales would like to meet me, so she gave us an introduction to one another and I was very very thrilled when he asked me for a dance. So I decided I would write down every word he said to me in my diary so I could always go back and read it over and over when I am really old. So then we started to dance and I asked him if he was still able to be fond of horses, and he said he was. So after our dance was all over he asked Dorothy for a dance but Dorothy will never learn how to act in front of a prince. Because she handed me her fan and she said "Hold this while I slip a new page into English histry," right in front of the Prince of Wales. So I was very very worried while Dorothy was dancing with the Prince of Wales because she talked to the Prince of Wales all the time and when she got through the Prince of Wales wrote some of the slang words she is always saying on his cuff, so if he tells the Queen some day to be 'a good Elk' or some other slang word Dorothy is always saying, the Queen will really blame me for bringing such a girl into English society. So when Dorothy came back we had quite a little quarrel because Dorothy said that since I met the Prince of Wales I was becoming too English. But really, I mean to say, I often remember papa back in Arkansas and he often used to say that his grandpa came from a place in England called Australia, so really, I mean to say, it is no wonder that the English seems to come out of me sometimes. Because if a girl seems to have an English accent I really think it is quite jolly.

April 20th:

Yesterday afternoon I really thought I ought to begin to educate Piggie how to act with a girl like American gentlemen act with a girl.

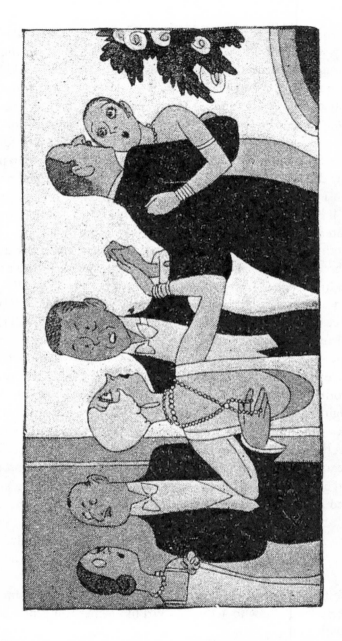

"So I asked the prince if he was still able to be fond of horses."

So I asked him to come up to have tea in our sitting room in the hotel because I had quite a headache. I mean I really look quite cute in my pink negligay. So I sent out a bell hop friend of Dorothy and I who is quite a nice boy who is called Harry and who we talk to quite a lot. So I gave Harry ten pounds of English money and I told him to go to the most expensive florist and to buy some very very expensive orchids for 10 pounds and to bring them to our sitting room at fifteen minutes past five and not to say a word but to say they were for me. So Piggie came to tea and we were having tea when Harry came in and he did not say a word but he gave me a quite large box and he said it was for me. So I opened the box and sure enough they were a dozen very very beautiful orchids. So I looked for a card, but of course there was no card so I grabbed Piggie and I said I would have to give him quite a large hug because it must have been him. But he said it was not him. But I said it must be him because I said that there was only one gentleman in London who was so sweet and generous and had such a large heart to send a girl one dozen orchids like him. So he still said it was not him. But I said I knew it was him, because there was not a gentleman in London so really marvelous and so wonderful and such a marvelous gentleman to send a girl one dozen orchids every day as him. So I really had to apologize for giving him such a large hug but I told him I was so full of impulses that when I knew he was going to send me one dozen orchids every day I became so impulsive I could not help it!

So then Dorothy and Gerald came in and I told them all about what a wonderful gentleman Piggie turned out to be and I told them when a gentleman sent a girl one dozen orchids every day he really reminded me of a prince. So Piggie blushed quite a lot and he was really very very pleased and he did not say any more that it was not him. So then I started to make a fuss over him and I told him he would have to look out because he was really so good looking and I was so full of impulses that I might even lose my mind some time and give him a kiss.

"I said I would have to give him quite a large hug."

So Piggie really felt very very good to be such a good looking gentleman. So he could not help blushing all the time and he could not help grinning all the time from one ear to another. So he asked us all to dinner and then he and Gerald went to change their clothes for dinner. So Dorothy and I had quite a little quarrel after they went because Dorothy asked me which one of the Jesse James brothers was my father. But I told her I was not so unrefined that I would waste my time with any gentleman who was only a ballroom dancer when he had a job. So Dorothy said Gerald was a gentleman because he wrote her a note and it had a crest. So I told her to try and eat it. So then we had to get dressed.

So this morning Harry, the boy friend of ours who is the bell hop, waked me up at ten o'clock because he had a box of one dozen orchids from Piggie. So by the time Piggie pays for a few dozen orchids, the diamond tiara will really seem like quite a bargain. Because I always think that spending money is only just a habit and if you get a gentleman started on buying one dozen orchids at a time he really gets very good habits.

April 21st:
Well, yesterday afternoon I took Piggie shopping on a street called Bond Street. So I took him to a jewelery store because I told him I had to have a silver picture frame because I had to have a picture of him to go in it. Because I told Piggie that when a girl gets to know such a good looking gentleman as him she really wants to have a picture of him on her dressing table where she can look at it a lot. So Piggie became quite intreeged. So we looked at all the silver picture frames. But then I told him that I really did not think a silver picture frame was good enough for a picture of him because I forgot that they had gold picture frames until I saw them. So then we started to look at the gold picture frames. So then it came out that his picture was taken in his unaform. So I said he must be so good looking in his unaform that I really did not think even the gold picture frames were

75

good enough but they did not have any platinum picture frames so we had to buy the best one we could.

So then I asked him if he could put on his unaform tomorrow because I would love to see him in his unaform and we could go to tea at Mrs. Weeks. So he really became very pleased because he grinned quite a lot and he said that he would. So then I said that poor little I would really look like nothing at all to be going out with him in his georgous unaform. So then we started to look at some bracelets but a lady friend of his who is quite friendly with his wife, who is in their country house in the country, came in to the store, so Piggie became quite nervous to be caught in a jewelery store where he has not been for years and years, so we had to go out.

This morning Gerald called up Dorothy and he said that day after tomorrow they are having a theatrical garden party to sell things to people for charity so he asked if Dorothy and I would be one of the ones who sells things to people for charity. So we said we would.

So now I must telephone Mrs. Weeks and say I will bring Sir Francis Beekman to tea tomorrow and I hope it all comes out all right. But I really wish Piggie would not tell so many storys. I mean I do not mind a gentleman when he tells a great many storys if they are new, but a gentleman who tells a great many storys and they are all the same storys is quite enervating. I mean London is really so uneducational that all I seem to be learning is some of Piggies storys and I even want to forget them. So I am really becoming jolly well fed up with London.

April 22nd:

Yesterday Piggie came in his unaform but he was really quite upset because he had a letter. I mean his wife is coming to London because she always comes to London every year to get her old clothes made over as she has a girl who does it very very cheap. So she is going to stay with the lady who saw us in the jewelery store, because it always saves money to stay with a friend. So I wanted to cheer Piggie up so I told him that I did not think the lady saw us and if she did see us, she really could not believe her eyes to see him in a jewelery store. But I did not tell him that I think that Dorothy and I had better go to Paris soon. Because, after all, Piggie's society is beginning to tell on a girls nerves. But I really made Piggie feel quite good about his unaform because I told him I only felt fit to be with him in a diamond tiara. So then I told him that, even if his wife was in London, we could still be friends, because I could not help but admire him even if his wife was in London and I told him I really thought a thing like that was nearly always the result of fate. So then we went to tea at Mrs. Weeks. So Piggie arranged with Mrs. Weeks to pay her for the diamond tiara and she nearly fell dead but she will keep it a secret because no one would believe it anyway. So now I have the diamond tiara and I have to admit that everything always turns out for the best. But I promised Piggie that I would always stay in London and we would always be friendly. Because Piggie always says that I am the only one who admires him for what he really is.

April 25th:

Well, we were so busy the last days I did not have time to write in my diary because now we are on a ship that seems to be quite a small ship to be sailing to Paris and we will be at Paris this afternoon. Because it does not take nearly so long to come to Paris as it does to come to London. I mean it seems quite unusual to think that it takes 6 days to come to London and only one day to come to Paris.

So Dorothy is quite upset because she did not want to come as she is madly in love with Gerald and Gerald said that we really ought not to leave London without going to see England while we happened to be here. But I told him that if England was the same kind of a place that London seems to be, I really know to much to bother with such a place.

"So I promised Piggie that I would always stay in London."

I mean we had quite a little quarrel because Gerald showed up at the station with a bangle for Dorothy so I told Dorothy she was well rid of such a person. So Dorothy had to come with me because Mr. Eisman is paying her expenses because he wants Dorothy to be my chaperone.

So the last thing in London was the garden party. I sold quite a lot of red baloons and I sold a red baloon to Harry Lauder the famous Scotch gentleman who is the famous Scotch tenor for 20 pounds. So Dorothy said I did not need to buy any ticket to Paris on the boat because if I could do that, I could walk across the channel.

So Piggy does not know that we have gone but I sent him a letter and told him I would see him some time again some time. And I was really glad to get out of our rooms at the Ritz—I mean 50 or 60 orchids really make a girl think of a funeral. So I cabled Mr. Eisman and I told him we could not learn anything in London because we knew to much, so if we went to Paris at least we could learn French, if we made up our mind to it.

So I am really very very intreeged as I have heard so much about Paris and I feel that it must be much more educational than London and I can hardly wait to see the Ritz hotel in Paris.

CHAPTER FOUR

PARIS IS DEVINE

April 27th:

Paris is devine. I mean Dorothy and I got to Paris yesterday, and it really is devine. Because the French are devine. Because when we were coming off the boat, and we were coming through the customs, it was quite hot and it seemed to smell quite a lot and all the French gentlemen in the customs, were squealing quite a lot. So I looked around and I picked out a French gentleman who was really in a very gorgeous uniform and he seemed to be a very, very important gentleman and I gave him twenty francs worth of French money and he was very very gallant and he knocked everybody else down and took our bags right through the custom. Because I really think that twenty Francs is quite cheap for a gentleman that has got on at least $100 worth of gold braid on his coat alone, to speak nothing of his trousers.

I mean the French gentlemen always seem to be squealing quite a lot, especially taxi drivers when they only get a small size yellow dime called a 'fifty santeems' for a tip. But the good thing about French gentlemen is that every time a French gentleman starts in to squeal, you can always stop him with five francs, no matter who he is. I mean it is so refreshing to listen to a French gentleman stop squeaking, that it would really be quite a bargain even for ten francs.

*"If you turn your back on a monument and
look up, you can see none other than Coty's sign!"*

So we came to the Ritz Hotel and the Ritz Hotel is devine. Because when a girl can sit in a delightful bar and have delicious champagne cocktails and look at all the important French people in Paris, I think it is devine. I mean when a girl can sit there and look at the Dolly sisters and Pearl White and Maybelle Gilman Corey, and Mrs. Nash, it is beyond worlds. Because when a girl looks at Mrs. Nash and realizes what Mrs. Nash has got out of gentlemen, it really makes a girl hold her breath.

And when a girl walks around and reads all of the signs with all of the famous historical names it really makes you hold your breath. Because when Dorothy and I went on a walk, we only walked a few blocks but in only a few blocks we read all of the famous historical names, like Coty and Cartier and I knew we were seeing something educational at last and our whole trip was not a failure. I mean I really try to make Dorothy get educated and have reverance. So when we stood at the corner of a place called the Place Vandome, if you turn your back on a monument they have in the middle and look up, you can see none other than Coty's sign. So I said to Dorothy, does it not really give you a thrill to realize that that is the historical spot where Mr. Coty makes all the perfume? So then Dorothy said that she supposed Mr. Coty came to Paris and he smelled Paris and he realized that something had to be done. So Dorothy will really never have any reverance.

So then we saw a jewelry store and we saw some jewelry in the window and it really seemed to be a very very great bargain but the price marks all had francs on them and Dorothy and I do not seem to be mathematical enough to tell how much francs is in money. So we went in and asked and it seems it was only 20 dollars and it seems it is not diamonds but it is a thing called "paste" which is the name of a word which means imitations.

So Dorothy said "paste" is the name of the word a girl ought to do to a gentleman that handed her one. I mean I would really be embarrassed, but the gentleman did not seem to understand Dorothy's english.

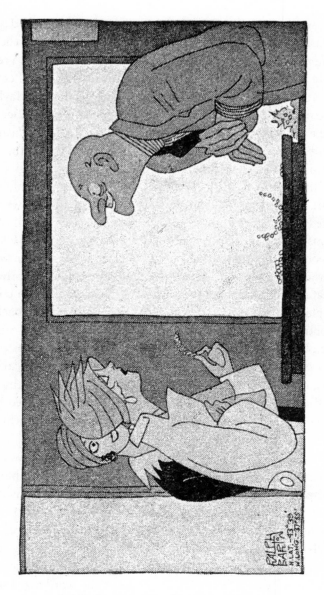

*"It really seemed to be a bargain but
Dorothy and I do not seem to be mathematical
enough to tell how much franks is in money."*

So it really makes a girl feel depressed to think a girl could not tell that it was nothing but an imitation. I mean a gentleman could deceeve a girl because he could give her a present and it would only be worth 20 dollars. So when Mr. Eisman comes to Paris next week, if he wants to make me a present I will make him take me along with him because he is really quite an inveteran bargain hunter at heart. So the gentleman at the jewelry store said that quite a lot of famous girls in Paris had imitations of all their jewelry and they put the jewelry in the safe and they really wore the imitations, so they could wear it and have a good time. But I told him I thought that any girl who was a lady would not even think of having such a good time that she did not remember to hang on to her jewelry.

So then we went back to the Ritz and unpacked our trunks with the aid of really a delightful waiter who brought us up some delicious luncheon and who is called Leon and who speaks english almost like an American and who Dorothy and I talk to quite a lot. So Leon said that we ought not to stay around the Ritz all of the time, but we really ought to see Paris. So Dorothy said she would go down in the lobby and meet some gentleman to show us Paris. So in a couple of minutes she called up on the telephone from the lobby and she said "I have got a French bird down here who is a French title nobleman, who is called a veecount so come on down." So I said "How did a Frenchman get into the Ritz." So Dorothy said "He came in to get out of the rain and he has not noticed that it is stopped." So I said "I suppose you have picked up something without taxi fare as usual. Why did you not get an American gentleman who always have money?" So Dorothy said she thought a French gentleman had ought to know Paris better. So I said "He does not even know it is not raining." But I went down.

So the veecount was really delightful after all. So then we rode around and we saw Paris and we saw how devine it really is. I mean the Eyefull Tower is devine and it is much more educational than the London Tower, because you can not even see the London Tower if you happen to be two blocks away. But when a girl looks at the Eyefull Tower she really knows she is looking at something. And it would even be very difficult not to notice the Eyefull Tower.

So then we went to a place called the Madrid to tea and it really was devine. I mean we saw the Dolley Sisters and Pearl White and Mrs. Corey and Mrs. Nash all over again.

So then we went to dinner and then we went to Momart and it really was devine because we saw them all over again. I mean in Momart they have genuine American jazz bands and quite a lot of New York people which we knew and you really would think you were in New York and it was devine. So we came back to the Ritz quite late. So Dorothy and I had quite a little quarrel because Dorothy said that when we were looking at Paris I asked the French veecount what was the name of the unknown soldier who is buried under quite a large monument. So I said I really did not mean to ask him, if I did, because what I did mean to ask him was, what was the name of his mother because it is always the mother of a dead soldier that I always seem to think about more than the dead soldier that has died.

So the French veecount is going to call up in the morning but I am not going to see him again. Because French gentlemen are really quite deceeving. I mean they take you to quite cute places and they make you feel quite good about yourself and you really seem to have a delightful time but when you get home and come to think it all over, all you have got is a fan that only cost 20 francs and a doll that they gave you away for nothing in a restaurant. I mean a girl has to look out in Paris, or she would have such a good time in Paris that she would not get anywheres. So I really think that American gentlemen are the best after all, because kissing your hand may make you feel very very good but a diamond and safire bracelet lasts forever.

*"Kissing your hand may make you feel
very good but a diamond bracelet lasts forever."*

Besides, I do not think that I ought to go out with any gentlemen in Paris because Mr. Eisman will be here next week and he told me that the only kind of gentlemen he wants me to go out with are intelectual gentlemen who are good for a girls brains. So I really do not seem to see many gentlemen around the Ritz who seem to look like they would be good for a girl's brains. So tomorrow we are going to go shopping and I suppose it would really be to much to expect to find a gentleman who would look to Mr. Eisman like he was good for a girls brains and at the same time he would like to take us shopping.

April 29th:
Yesterday was quite a day. I mean Dorothy and I were getting ready to go shopping and the telephone rang and they said that Lady Francis Beekman was down stairs and she wanted to come up stairs. So I really was quite surprised. I mean I did not know what to say, so I said all right. So then I told Dorothy and then we put our brains together. Because it seems that Lady Francis Beekman is the wife of the gentleman called Sir Francis Beekman who was the admirer of mine in London who seemed to admire me so much that he asked me if he could make me a present of a diamond tiara. So it seemed as if his wife must have heard about it, and it really seemed as if she must have come clear over from London about it. So there was a very very loud knock at the door so we asked her to come in. So Lady Francis Beekman came in and she is a quite large size lady who seems to resemble Bill Hart quite a lot. I mean Dorothy thinks that Lady Francis Beeckman resembles Bill Hart quite a lot, only she really thinks she looks more like Bill Hart's horse. So it seems that she said that if I did not give her back the diamond tiara right away, she would make quite a fuss and she would ruin my reputation. Because she said that something really must be wrong about the whole thing. Because it seems that Sir Francis Beekman and she have been married for 35 years and the last present he gave to her was a wedding ring.

*"Dorothy said 'You have got to be the Queen
of England to get away with a hat like that.'"*

So Dorothy spoke up and she said "Lady you could no more ruin my girl friends reputation than you could sink the Jewish fleet." I mean I was quite proud of Dorothy the way she stood up for my reputation. Because I really think that there is nothing so wonderful as two girls when they stand up for each other and help each other a lot. Because no matter how vigarous Lady Francis Beekman seems to be, she had to realize that she could not sink a whole fleet full of ships. So she had to stop talking against my reputation.

So then she said she would drag it into the court and she would say that it was undue influence. So I said to her, "If you wear that hat into a court, we will see if the judge thinks it took an undue influence to make Sir Francis Beekman look at a girl." So then Dorothy spoke up and Dorothy said "My girl friend is right, Lady. You have got to be the Queen of England to get away with a hat like that." So Lady Francis Beekman seemed to get quite angry. So then she said she would send for Sir Francis Beekman where he suddenly went to Scotland, to go hunting when he found out that Lady Francis Beekman had found out. So Dorothy said "Do you mean that you have left Sir Francis Beekman loose with all those spendthrifts down in Scotland?" So Dorothy said she would better look out or he would get together with the boys some night and simply massacre a haypenny. I mean I always encouradge Dorothy to talk quite a lot when we are talking to unrefined people like Lady Francis Beekman, because Dorothy speaks their own languadge to unrefined people better than a refined girl like I. So Dorothy said, "You had better not send for Sir Francis Beekman because if my girl friend really wanted to turn loose on Sir Francis Beekman, all he would have left would be his title." So then I spoke right up and said Yes that I was an American girl and we American girls do not care about a title because we American girls always say that what is good enough for Washington is good enough for us. So Lady Francis Beekman really seemed to get more angry and more angry all of the time.

So then she said that if it was necessary, she would tell the judge that Sir Francis Beekman went out of his mind when he gave it to me. So Dorothy said "Lady, if you go into a court and if the judge gets a good look at you, he will think that Sir Francis Beekman was out of his mind 35 years ago." So then Lady Francis Beekman said she knew what kind of a person she had to deal with and she would not deal with any such a person because she said it hurt her dignity. So Dorothy said "Lady, if we hurt your dignity like you hurt our eyesight I hope for your sake, you are a Christian science." So that seemed to make Lady Francis Beekman angry. So she said she would turn it all over to her soliciter. So when she went out she tripped over quite a long train which she had on her skirt and she nearly fell down. So Dorothy leaned out of the door and Dorothy called down the hall and said, "Take a tuck in that skirt Isabel, its 1925." So I really felt quite depressed because I felt as if our whole morning was really very unrefined just because we had to mix with such an unrefined lady as Lady Francis Beekman.

April 30th:

So sure enough yesterday morning Lady Francis Beekman's solicitor came. Only he really was not a solicitor, but his name was on a card and it seems his name is Mons. Broussard and it seems that he is an advocat because an advocat is a lawyer in the French landguage. So Dorothy and I were getting dressed and we were in our negligay as usual when there was quite a loud knock on the door and before we could even say come in he jumped right into the room. So it seems that he is of French extraction. I mean Lady Francis Beekman's solicitor can really squeal just like a taxi driver. I mean he was squealing quite loud when he jumped into the room and he kept right on squealing. So Dorothy and I rushed into the parlor and Dorothy looked at him and Dorothy said, "This town has got to stop playing jokes on us every morning" because our nerves could not stand it. So Mons. Broussard handed us his card and he squealed and squealed and he really waved his arms in the air quite a lot. So Dorothy said He gives quite a good imitation of the Moulan Rouge, which is really a red wind mill, only Dorothy said he makes more noise and he runs on his own wind. So we stood and watched him for quite a long while, but he seemed to get quite monotonous after quite a long while because he was always talking in French, which really means nothing to us. So Dorothy said "Lets see if 25 francs will stop him, because if 5 francs will stop a taxi driver, 25 francs ought to stop an advocat." Because he was making about 5 times as much noise as a taxi driver and 5 times 5 is 25. So as soon as he heard us start in to talk about francs he seemed to calm down quite a little. So Dorothy got her pocket book and she gave him 25 francs. So then he stopped squealing and he put it in his pocket, but then he got out quite a large size handkerchief with purple elefants on it and he started in to cry. So Dorothy really got discouraged and she said, "Look here, you have given us a quite an amusing morning but if you keep that up much longer, wet or dry, out you go."

So then he started in to pointing at the telephone and he seemed to want to use the telephone and Dorothy said, "If you think you can get a number over that thing, go to it, but as far as we have found out, it is a wall bracket." So then he started in to telephone so Dorothy and I went about our business to get dressed. So when he finished telephoning he kept running to my door and then he kept running to Dorothy's door, and he kept on crying and talking a lot, but he seemed to have lost all of his novelty to us so we paid no more attention to him.

So finally there was another loud knock on the door so we heard him rush to the door so we both went in to the parlor to see what it was and it really was a sight. Because it was another Frenchman. So the new Frenchman rushed in and he yelled Papa and he kissed him. So it seems that it was his son because his son is really his papa's partner in the advocat business. So then his papa talked quite a lot and then he pointed at I and Dorothy. So then his son looked at us and then his son let out quite a large size squeal, and he said in French "May papa, elles sont sharmant." So it seems he was telling his papa in French that we were really charming. So then Mons. Broussard stopped crying and put on his glasses and took a good look at us. So then his son put up the window shade, so his papa could get a better look at us. So when his papa had finished looking at us he really became delighted. So he became all smiles and he pinched our cheeks and he kept on saying Sharmant all of the time because Sharmant means charming in the French languadge. So then his son broke right out into english and he really speaks english as good as an American. So then he told us his papa telephoned for him to come over because we did not seem to understand what his papa was saying to us. So it seems that Mons. Broussard had been talking to us in english all of the time but we did not seem to understand his kind of english. So Dorothy said, "If what your papa was talking in was english, I could get a gold medal for my greek." So then his son told his papa and his papa laughed very very loud and he pinched Dorothys cheek and he was very delighted even if the joke was on him. So then Dorothy and I asked his son what he was saying, when he was talking to us in english and his son said he was telling us all about his client, Lady Francis Beekman. So then we asked his son why his papa kept crying. So then his son said his papa kept crying because he was thinking about Lady Francis Beekman. So Dorothy said, "If he cries when he thinks about her, what does he do when he looks at her?" So then his son explained to his papa what Dorothy said. So then Mons. Broussard laughed very very loud, so then he kissed Dorothy's hand, so he said, after that, we would all really have to have a bottle of champagne. So he went to the telephone and ordered a bottle of champagne.

So then his son said to his papa, "Why do we not ask the charming ladies to go out to Fountainblo to-day." So his papa said it would be charming. So then I said, "How are we going to tell you gentlemen apart, because if it is the same in Paris as it is in America, you would both seem to be Monshure Broussard."

So then we got the idea to call them by their first name. So it seems that his son's name is Louie so Dorothy spoke up and said, "I hear that they number all of you Louies over here in Paris." Because a girl is always hearing some one talk about Louie the sixteenth who seemed to be in the anteek furniture business. I mean I was surprised to hear Dorothy get so historical so she may really be getting educated in spite of everything. But Dorothy told Louie he need not try to figure out his number because she got it the minute she looked at him. So it seems his papa's name is Robber, which means Robert in French. So Dorothy started in to think about her 25 francs and she said to Robber, "Your mother certainly knew her grammer when she called you that."

So Dorothy said we might as well go out to Fountainblo with Louie and Robber if Louie would take off his yellow spats that were made out of yellow shammy skin with pink pearl buttons. Because Dorothy said, "Fun is fun but no girl wants to laugh all of the time." So Louie is really always anxious to please, so he took off his spats but when he took off his spats, we saw his socks and when we saw his socks we saw that they were Scotch plaid with small size rainbows running through them. So Dorothy looked at them a little while and she really became quite discouraged and she said, "Well Louie, I think you had better put your spats back on."

So then Leon, our friend who is the waiter, came in with the bottle of champagne. So while he was opening the bottle of champagne Louie and Robber talked together in French quite a lot and I really think I had ought to find out what they said in French because it might be about the diamond tiara. Because French gentlemen are very very gallant, but I really do not think a girl can trust one of them around a corner. So, when I get a chance, I am going to ask Leon what they said.

So then we went to Fountainblo and then we went to Momart and we got home very late, and we really had quite a delightful day and night, even if we did not go out shopping and buy anything. But I really think we ought to do more shopping because shopping really seems to be what Paris is principaly for.

May 1st:

Well this morning I sent for Leon, who is Dorothy and my waiter friend, and I asked him what Louie and Robber said in French. So it seems that they said in French that we seemed to attract them very very much because they really thought that we were very very charming, and they had not met girls that were so charming in quite a long time. So it seems that they said that they would ask us out a lot and that they would charge up all the bills to Lady Francis Beekman because they would watch for their chance and they would steal the diamond tiara. So then they said that even if they could not steal it from us, we were really so charming that it would be delightful to go around with us, even if they could not steal from us. So no matter what happens they really could not lose. Because it seems that Lady Francis Beekman would be glad to pay all the bills when they told her they had to take us out a lot so they could watch for their chance and steal it. Because Lady Francis Beekman is the kind of a wealthy lady that does not spend money on anything else but she will always spend money on a law suit. And she really would not mind spending the money because it seems that something either I or Dorothy said to Lady Francis Beekman seemed to make her angry.

So then I decided it was time to do some thinking and I really thought quite a lot. So I told Dorothy I thought I would put the real diamond tiara in the safe at the Ritz and then I would buy an imitation of a diamond tiara at the jewelry store that has the imitations that are called paste. So then I would leave the imitation of the diamond tiara lying around, so Louie and Robber could see how careless I seem to be with it so then they would get full of encouradgement. So when we go out with Louie and Robber I could put it in my hand bag and I could take it with me so Louie and Robber could always feel that the diamond tiara was within reach. So then Dorothy and I could get them to go shopping and we could get them to spend quite a lot and every time they seemed to get discouradged, I could open my hand bag, and let them get a glimpse of the imitation of a diamond tiara and they would become more encouradged and then they would spend some more money. Because I even might let them steal it at the last, because they were really charming gentlemen after all and I really would like to help Louie and Robber. I mean it would be quite amusing for them to steal it for Lady Francis Beekman and she would have to pay them quite a lot and then she would find out it was only made out of paste after all. Because Lady Francis Beekman has never seen the real diamond tiara and the imitation of a diamond tiara would really deceive her, at least until Louie and Robber got all of their money for all of the hard work they did. I mean the imitation of a diamond tiara would only cost about 65 dollars and what is 65 dollars if Dorothy and I could do some delightful shopping and get some delightful presents that would even seem more delightful when we stopped to realize that Lady Francis Beekman paid for them. And it would teach Lady Francis Beekman a lesson not to say what she said to two American girls like I and Dorothy, who were all alone in Paris and had no gentleman to protect them.

So when I got through telling Dorothy what I thought up, Dorothy looked at me and looked at me and she really said she thought my brains were a miracle. I mean she said my brains reminded her of a radio because you listen to it for days and days and you get discouradged and just when you are getting ready to smash it, something comes out that is a masterpiece.

So then Louie called us up so Dorothy told him that we thought it would be delightful if he and Robber would take us out shopping tomorrow morning. So then Louie asked his papa and his papa said they would. So then they asked us if we would like to go to see a play called The Foley Bergere tonight. So he said that all of the French people who live in Paris are always delighted to have some Americans, so it will give them an excuse to go to the Foley Bergere. So we said we would go. So now Dorothy and I are going out shopping to buy the imitation of a diamond tiara and we are going out window shopping to pick out where we would like Louie and Robber to take us shopping tomorrow. So I really think that everything always works out for the best. Because after all, we really need some gentlemen to take us around until Mr. Eisman gets to Paris and we could not go around with any really attractive gentlemen because Mr. Eisman only wants me to go out with gentlemen that have brains. So I said to Dorothy that, even if Louie and Robber do not look so full of brains, we could tell Mr. Eisman that all we were learning from them was French. So even if I have not seemed to learn French yet, I have really almost learned to understand Robbers english so when Robber talks in front of Mr. Eisman and I seem to understand what he is saying, Mr. Eisman will probably think I know French.

May 2nd:
So last night we went to the Foley Bergere and it really was devine. I mean it was very very artistic because it had girls in it that were in the nude. So one of the girls was a friend of Louie and he said that she was a very very nice girl, and that she was only 18 years of age. So Dorothy said, "She is slipping it over on you Louie, because how could a girl get such dirty knees in only 18 years?" So Louie and Robber really laughed very very loud. I mean Dorothy was very unrefined at the Foley Bergere. But I always think that when girls are in the nude it is very artistic and if you have artistic thoughts you think it is beautiful and I really would not laugh in an artistic place like the Foley Bergere.

So I wore the imitation of a diamond tiara to the Foley Bergere. I mean it really would deceeve an expert and Louie and Robber could hardly take their eyes off of it. But they did not really annoy me because I had it tied on very very tight. I mean it would be fatal if they got the diamond tiara before Dorothy and I took them shopping a lot.

"Dorothy was very unrefined at the Foley Bergere."

So we are all ready to go shopping this morning and Robber was here bright and early and he is in the parlor with Dorothy and we are waiting for Louie. So I left the daimond tiara on the table in the parlor so Robber could see how careless I really am with everything but Dorothy is keeping her eye on Robber. So I just heard Louie come in because I heard him kissing Robber. I mean Louie is always kissing Robber and Dorothy told Louie that if he did not stop kissing Robber, people would think that he painted batiks.

So now I must join the others and I will put the diamond tiara in my hand bag so that Louie and Robber will feel that it is always around and we will all go shopping. And I almost have to smile when I think of Lady Francis Beekman.

May 3rd:
Yesterday was really delightful. I mean Louie and Robber bought Dorothy and I some delightful presents. But then they began to run out of all the franks they had with them, so they began to get discouradged but just as soon as they began to get discouradged, I gave Robber my hand bag to hold while I went to the fitting room to try on a blouse. So he was cheered up quite a lot, but of course Dorothy stayed with them and kept her eye on Robber so he did not get a chance. But it really cheered him up quite a lot to even hold it.

So after all their franks were gone, Robber said he would have to telephone to some one, so I suppose he telephoned to Lady Francis Beekman and she must have said All right because Robber left us at a place called the Cafe de la Paix because he had to go on an errand and when he came back from his errand he seemed to have quite a lot more franks. So then they took us to luncheon so that after luncheon we could go out shopping some more.

But I am really learning quite a lot of French in spite of everything. I mean if you want delicious chicken and peas for luncheon all you have to say is "pettypas" and "pulle." I mean

French is really very easy, for instance the French use the word "sheik" for everything, while we only seem to use it for gentlemen when they seem to resemble Rudolf Valentino.

So while we were shopping in the afternoon I saw Louie get Dorothy off in a corner and whisper to her quite a lot. So then I saw Robber get her off in a corner and whisper to her quite a lot. So when we got back to the Ritz, Dorothy told me why they whispered to her. So it seems when Louie whispered to Dorothy, Louie told Dorothy that if she would steal the diamond tiara from me and give it to him and not let his papa know, he would give her 1000 franks. Because it seems that Lady Francis Beekman has got her heart set on it and she will pay quite a lot for it because she is quite angry and when she really gets as angry as she is, she is only a woman with one idea. So if Louie could get it and his papa would not find it out, he could keep all the money for himself. So it seems that later on, when Robber was whispering to Dorothy, he was making her the same proposition for 2000 franks so that Louie would not find out and Robber could keep all the money for himself. So I really think it would be delightful if Dorothy could make some money for herself because it might make Dorothy get some ambishions. So tomorrow morning Dorothy is going to take the diamond tiara and she is going to tell Louie that she stole it and she is going to sell it to Louie. But she will make him hand over the money first and then, just as she is going to hand over the diamond tiara, I am going to walk in on them and say, "Oh there is my diamond tiara. I have been looking for it everywhere." So then I will get it back. So then she will tell him that she might just as well keep the 1000 franks because she will steal it for him again in the afternoon. So in the afternoon she is going to sell it to Robber and I really think we will let Robber keep it. Because I am quite fond of Robber. I mean he is quite a sweet old gentleman and it is really refreshing the way he and his son love one another. Because even if it is unusual for an American to see a French gentleman always kissing his father, I really think it is refreshing and I think that we Americans would be better off if we American fathers and sons would love one another more like Louie and Robber.

So Dorothy and I have quite a lot of delightful hand bags and stockings and handkerchiefs and scarfs and things and some quite cute models of evening gowns that are all covered with imitations of diamonds, only they do not call them "paste" when they are on a dress but they call them "diamonteys" and I really think a girl looks quite cute when she is covered all over with "diamonteys."

May 5th:

So yesterday morning Dorothy sold the imitation of a diamond tiara to Louie. So then we got it back. So in the afternoon we all went out to Versigh. I mean Louie and Robber were quite delighted not to go shopping any more so I suppose that Lady Francis Beekman really thinks that there is a limit to almost everything. So I took Louie for a walk at Versigh so that Dorothy would have a chance to sell it to Robber. So then she sold it to Robber. So then he put it in his pocket. But when we were coming home I got to thinking things over and I really got to thinking that an imitation of a diamond tiara was quite a good thing to have after all. I mean especially if a girl goes around a lot in Paris, with admirers who are of the French extraction. And after all, I really do not think a girl ought to encouradge Robber to steal something from two American girls who are all alone in Paris and have no gentleman to protect them. So I asked Dorothy which pocket Robber put it in, so I sat next to him in the automobile coming home and I took it out.

So we were in quite a quaint restaurant for dinner when Robber put his hand in his pocket and then he started in to squeal once more. So it seems he had lost something, so he and Louie had one of their regular squealing and shoulder shrugging matches.

"So then Robber started in to squeal once more."

But Louie told his papa that he did not steal it out of his papa's pocket. But then Robber started in to cry to think that his son would steal something out of his own papa's pocket. So after Dorothy and I had had about all we could stand, I told them all about it. I mean I really felt sorry for Robber so I told him not to cry any more because it was nothing but paste after all. So then I showed it to them. So then Louie and Robber looked at Dorothy and I and they really held their breath. So I suppose that most of the girls in Paris do not have such brains as we American girls.

So after it was all over, Louie and Robber seemed to be so depressed that I really felt sorry for them. So I got an idea. So I told them that we would all go out tomorrow to the imitation of a jewelry store and they could buy another imitation of a diamond tiara to give to Lady Francis Beekman and they could get the man in the jewelry store to put on the bill that it was a hand bag and they could charge the bill to Lady Francis Beekman along with the other expenses. Because Lady Francis Beekman had never seen the real diamond tiara anyway. So Dorothy spoke up and Dorothy said that as far as Lady Francis Beekman would know about diamonds, you could nick off a piece of ice and give it to her, only it would melt. So then Robber looked at me and looked at me, and he reached over and kissed me on the forehead in a way that was really full of reverance.

So then we had quite a delightful evening. I mean because we all seem to understand one another because, after all, Dorothy and I could really have a platonick friendship with gentlemen like Louie and Robber. I mean there seems to be something common between us, especially when we all get to thinking about Lady Francis Beekman.

So they are going to charge Lady Francis Beekman quite a lot of money when they give her the imitation of a diamond tiara and I told Robber if she seems to complane, to ask her, if she knew that Sir Francis Beekman sent me 10 pounds worth of orchids every day while we were in London. So that would make her so angry that she would be glad to pay almost anything to

103

get the diamond tiara.

So when Lady Francis Beekman pays them all the money, Louie and Robber are going to give us a dinner in our honor at Ciros. So when Mr. Eisman gets here on Saturday, Dorothy and I are going to make Mr. Eisman give Louie and Robber a dinner in their honor at Ciros because of the way they helped us when we were two American girls all alone in Paris and could not even speak the French landguage.

So Louie and Robber asked us to come to a party at their sister's house today but Dorothy says we had better not go because it is raining and we both have brand new umbrellas that are quite cute and Dorothy says she would not think of leaving a brand new umbrella in a French lady's hall and it is no fun to hang on to an umbrella all the time you are at a party. So we had better be on the safe side and stay away. So we called up Louie and told him we had a headache but we thanked him for all of his hospitality. Because it is the way all the French people like Louie and Robber are so hospitable to we Americans that really makes Paris so devine.

CHAPTER FIVE

THE CENTRAL OF EUROPE

May 16th:

I really have not written in my diary for quite a long time, because Mr. Eisman arrived in Paris and when Mr. Eisman is in Paris we really do not seem to do practically anything else but the same thing.

I mean we go shopping and we go to a show and we go to Momart and when a girl is always going with Mr. Eisman nothing practically happens. And I did not even bother to learn any more French because I always seem to think it is better to leave French to those that can not do anything else but talk French. So finally Mr. Eisman seemed to lose quite a lot of interest in all of my shopping. So he heard about a button factory that was for sale quite cheaply in Vienna and as Mr. Eisman is in the button profession, he thought it would be a quite good thing to have a button factory in Vienna so he went to Vienna and he said he did not care if he did not ever see the rue de la Paix again. So he said if he thought Vienna would be good for a girl's brains, he would send for Dorothy and I and we could meet him at Vienna and learn something. Because Mr. Eisman really wants me to get educated more than anything else, especially shopping.

So now we have a telegram, and Mr. Eisman says in the telegram for Dorothy and I to take an oriental express because we really ought to see the central of Europe because we American girls have quite a lot to learn in the central of Europe.

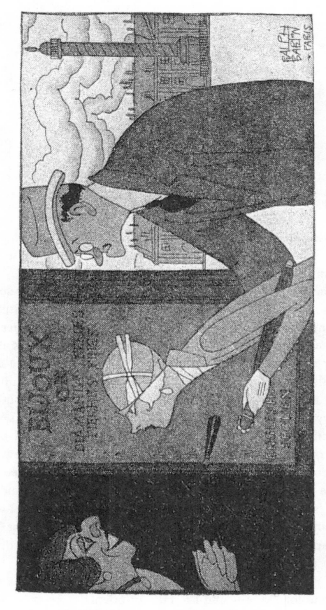

*"When Mr. Eisman is in Paris we do
not do anything else but the same thing."*

So Dorothy says if Mr. Eisman wants us to see the central of Europe she bets there is not a rue de la Paix in the whole central of Europe.

So Dorothy and I are going to take an oriental express tomorrow and I really think it is quite unusual for two American girls like I and Dorothy to take an oriental express all alone, because it seems that in the Central of Europe they talk some other kinds of landguages which we do not understand besides French. But I always think that there is nearly always some gentleman who will protect two American girls like I and Dorothy who are all alone and who are traveling in the Central of Europe to get educated.

May 17th:

So now we are on an oriental express and everything seems to be quite unusual. I mean Dorothy and I got up this morning and we looked out of the window of our compartment and it was really quite unusual. Because it was farms, and we saw quite a lot of girls who seemed to be putting small size hay stacks onto large size hay stacks while their husbands seemed to sit at a table under quite a shady tree and drink beer. Or else their husbands seemed to sit on a fence and smoke their pipe and watch them. So Dorothy and I looked at two girls who seemed to be ploughing up all of the ground with only the aid of a cow and Dorothy said, "I think we girls have gone one step to far away from New York, because it begins to look to me as if the Central of Europe is no country for we girls." So we both became quite worried. I mean I became quite depressed because if this is what Mr. Eisman thinks we American girls ought to learn I really think it is quite depressing. So I do not think we care to meet any gentlemen who have been born and raised in the Central of Europe. I mean the more I travel and the more I seem to see other gentlemen the more I seem to think of American gentlemen.

So now I am going to get dressed and go to the dining car and look for some American gentleman and hold a conversation, because I really feel so depressed. I mean Dorothy keeps trying to depress me because she keeps saying that I will probably end up in a farm in the Central of Europe doing a sister act with a plough. Because Dorothy's jokes are really very unrefined and I think that I will feel much better if I go to the dining car and have some luncheon.

Well I went to the dining car and I met a gentleman who was quite a delightful American gentleman, I mean it was quite a co-instance, because we girls have always heard about Henry Spoffard and it was really nobody else but the famous Henry Spoffard, who is the famous Spoffard family, who is a very very fine old family who is very very wealthy. I mean Mr. Spoffard is one of the most famous familys in New York and he is not like most gentlemen who are wealthy, but he works all of the time for the good of the others. I mean he is the gentleman who always gets his picture in all of the newspapers because he is always senshuring all of the plays that are not good for peoples morals. And all of we girls remember the time when he was in the Ritz for luncheon and he met a gentleman friend of his and the gentleman friend had Peggy Hopkins Joyce to luncheon and he introduced Peggy Hopkins Joyce to Mr. Spoffard and Mr. Spoffard turned on his heels and walked away. Because Mr. Spoffard is a very very famous Prespyterian and he is really much to Prespyterian to meet Peggy Hopkins Joyce. I mean it is unusual to see a gentleman who is such a young gentleman as Mr. Spoffard be so Prespyterian, because when most gentlemen are 35 years of age their minds nearly always seem to be on something else.

So when I saw no one else but the famous Mr. Spoffard I really became quite thrilled. Because all of we girls have tried very hard to have an introduction to Henry Spoffard and it was quite unusual to be shut up on a train in the Central of Europe with him. So I thought it would be quite unusual for a girl like I to have a friendship with a gentleman like Mr. Spoffard, who really does not even look at a girl unless she at least looks like a

Prespyterian. And I mean our family in Little Rock were really not so Prespyterians.

So I thought I would sit at his table. So then I had to ask him about all of the money because all of the money they use in the Central of Europe has not even got so much sense to it as the kind of franks they use in Paris. Because it seems to be called kronens and it seems to take quite a lot of them because it takes 50,000 of them to even buy a small size package of cigarettes and Dorothy says if the cigarettes had tobacco in them, we couldn't lift enough kronens over a counter to pay for a package. So this morning Dorothy and I asked the porter to bring us a bottle of champagne and we really did not know what to give him for a tip. So Dorothy said for me to take one of the things called a one million kronens and she would take one of them called a one million kronens and I would give him mine first and if he gave me quite a dirty look, she would give him hers. So after we paid for the bottle of champagne I gave him my one million kronens and before we could do anything else he started in to grabbing my hand and kissing my hand and getting down on his knees. So we finally had to push him right out of the compartment. So one million kronens seemed to be enough. So I told Mr. Spoffard how we did not know what to give the porter when he brought us our bottle of minral water. So then I asked him to tell me all about all of the money because I told him I always seem to think that a penny earned was a penny saved. So it really was quite unusual because Mr. Spoffard said that that was his favorite motto.

So then we got to talking quite a lot and I told him that I was traveling to get educated and I told him I had a girl with me who I was trying to reform because I thought if she would put her mind more on getting educated, she would get more reformed. Because after all Mr. Spoffard will have to meet Dorothy sooner or later and he might wonder what a refined girl like I was doing with a girl like Dorothy. So Mr. Spoffard really became quite intreeged. Because Mr. Spoffard loves to reform people and he loves to senshure everything and he really came over to Europe to look at all the things that Americans come over to Europe to look at, when they really should not look at them but they should look at all of the museums instead. Because if that is all we Americans come to Europe to look at, we should stay home and look at America first. So Mr. Spoffard spends all of his time looking at things that spoil peoples morals. So Mr. Spoffard really must have very very strong morals or else all the things that spoil other peoples morals would spoil his morals. But they do not seem to spoil Mr. Spoffards morals and I really think it is wonderful to have such strong morals. So I told Mr. Spoffard that I thought that civilization is not what it ought to be and we really ought to have something else to take its place.

So Mr. Spoffard said that he would come to call on Dorothy and I in our compartment this afternoon and we would talk it all over, if his mother does not seem to need him in her compartment. Because Mr. Spoffards mother always travels with Mr. Spoffard and he never does anything unless he tells his mother all about it, and asks his mother if he ought to. So he told me that that is the reason he has never got married, because his mother does not think that all of the flappers we seem to have nowadays are what a young man ought to marry when a young man is full of so many morals as Mr. Spoffard seems to be full of. So I told Mr. Spoffard that I really felt just like his mother feels about all of the flappers because I am an old fashioned girl.

So then I got to worrying about Dorothy quite a lot because Dorothy is really not so old-fashioned and she might say something in front of Mr. Spoffard that might make Mr. Spoffard wonder what such an old-fashioned girl as I was doing with such a girl as Dorothy. So I told him how I was having quite a hard time reforming Dorothy and I would like to have him meet Dorothy so he could tell me if he really thinks I am wasting quite a lot of time trying to reform a girl like Dorothy. So then he had to go to his mother. So I really hope that Dorothy will act more reformed than she usually acts in front of Mr. Spoffard.

Well Mr. Spoffard just left our compartment so he really came to pay a call on us after all. So Mr. Spoffard told us all about his mother and I was really very very intreeged because if Mr. Spoffard and I become friendly he is the kind of a gentleman that always wants a girl to meet his mother. I mean if a girl gets to know what kind of a mother a gentlemans mother is like, she really knows more what kind of a conversation to use on a gentleman's mother when she meets her. Because a girl like I is really always on the verge of meeting gentlemen's mothers. But such an unrefined girl as Dorothy is really not the kind of a girl that ever meets gentlemens mothers.

So Mr. Spoffard says his mother has to have him take care of her quite a lot. Because Mr. Spoffards mothers brains have never really been so strong. Because it seems his mother came from such a very fine old family that even when she was quite a small size child she had to be sent to a school that was a special school for people of very fine old familys who had to have things very easy on their brain. So she still has to have things very easy on her brain, so she has a girl who is called her companion who goes with her everywhere who is called Miss Chapman. Because Mr. Spoffard says that there is always something new going on in the world which they did not get a chance to tell her about at the school. So now Miss Chapman keeps telling her instead. Because how would she know what to think about such a new thing as a radio, for instance, if she did not have Miss Chapman to tell her what it was, for instance. So Dorothy spoke up and Dorothy said, "What a responsibility that girl has got on her shoulders. For instance, what if Miss Chapman told her a radio was something to build a fire in, and she would get cold some day and stuff it full of papers and light it." But Mr. Spoffard told Dorothy that Miss Chapman would never make such a mistake. Because he said that Miss Chapman came from a very very fine old family herself and she really had a fine brain. So Dorothy said, "If she really has got such a fine brain I bet her fine old family once had an ice man who could not be trusted." So Mr. Spoffard and I did

111

not pay any more attention to Dorothy because Dorothy really does not know how to hold a conversation.

So then I and Mr. Spoffard held a conversation all about morals and Mr. Spoffard says he really thinks the future of everything is between the hands of Mr. Blank the district attorney who is the famous district attorney who is closing up all the places in New York where they sell all of the liquor. So Mr. Spoffard said that a few months ago, when Mr. Blank decided he would try to get the job to be the district attorney, he put 1,000 dollars worth of liquor down his sink. So now Mr. Blank says that everybody else has got to put it down their sink. So Dorothy spoke up, and Dorothy said, "If he poured 1,000 dollars worth down his sink to get himself one million dollars worth of publicity and a good job—when we pour it down our sink, what do we get?" But Mr. Spoffard is to brainy a gentleman to answer any such a foolish question. So he gave Dorothy a look that was full of dignity and he said he would have to go back to his Mother. So I was really quite angry at Dorothy. So I followed Mr. Spoffard down the hall of the railway train and I asked Mr. Spoffard if he thought I was wasting quite a lot of time reforming a girl like Dorothy. So Mr. Spoffard thinks I am, because he really thinks a girl like Dorothy will never have any reverance. So I told Mr. Spoffard I had wasted so much time on Dorothy it would really break my heart to be a failure. So then I had tears in my eyes. So Mr. Spoffard is really very very sympathetic because when he saw that I did not have any handkerchief, he took his own handkerchief and he dried up all of my tears. So then he said he would help me with Dorothy quite a lot and get her mind to running on things that are more educational.

So then he said he thought that we ought to get off the train at a place called Munich because it was very full of art, which they call "kunst" in Munich, which is very, very educational. So he said he and Dorothy and I would get off of the train in Munich because he could send his mother right on to Vienna with Miss Chapman, because every place always seems to look alike to his mother anyway. So we are all going to get off the train at Munich and I can send Mr. Eisman a telegram when nobody is looking. Because I really do not think I will tell Mr. Spoffard about Mr. Eisman, because, after all, their religions are different and when two gentlemen have such different religions they do not seem to have so much to get congeneal about. So I can telegraph Mr. Eisman that Dorothy and I thought we would get off the train at Munich to look at all of the art.

So then I went back to Dorothy and I told Dorothy if she did not have anything to say in the future to not say it. Because even if Mr. Spoffard is a fine old family and even if he is very Prespyterian, I and he could really be friendly after all and talk together quite a lot. I mean Mr. Spoffard likes to talk about himself quite a lot, so I said to Dorothy it really shows that, after all, he is just like any other gentleman. But Dorothy said she would demand more proof than that. So Dorothy says she thinks that maybe I might become quite friendly with Mr. Spoffard and especially with his mother because she thinks his mother and I have quite a lot that is common, but she says, if I ever bump into Miss Chapman, she thinks I will come to a kropper because Dorothy saw Miss Chapman when she was at luncheon and Dorothy says Miss Chapman is the kind of a girl that wears a collar and a tie even when she is not on horseback. And Dorothy said it was the look that Miss Chapman gave her at luncheon that really gave her the idea about the ice man. So Dorothy says she thinks Miss Chapman has got 3 thirds of the brains of that trio of Geegans, because Geegans is the slang word that Dorothy has thought up to use on people who are society people. Because Dorothy says she thinks any gentleman with Mr. Spoffards brains had ought to spend his time putting nickels into an electric piano, but I did not even bother to talk back at such a girl as Dorothy. So now we must get ready to get off the train when the train gets to Munich so that we can look at all of the kunst in Munich.

*"The Germans stand in the lobby of the theatre and
eat quite a lot of Bermudian onions and garlick sausage."*

114

May 19th:

Well yesterday Mr. Spoffard and I and Dorothy got off the train at Munich to see all of the kunst in Munich, but you only call it Munich when you are on the train because as soon as you get off of the train they seem to call it Munchen. So you really would know that Munchen was full of kunst because in case you would not know it, they have painted the word "kunst" in large size black letters on everything in Munchen, and you can not even see a boot black's stand in Munchen that is not full of kunst.

So Mr. Spoffard said that we really ought to go to the theater in Munchen because even the theater in Munchen was full of kunst. So we looked at all of the bills of all of the theaters, with the aid of quite an intelectual hotel clerk who seemed to be able to read it and tell us what it said, because it really meant nothing to us. So it seems they were playing Kiki in Munchen, so I said, let us go and see Kiki because we have seen Lenore Ulric in New York and we would really know what it is all about even if they do not seem to talk the English landguage. So then we went to the Kunst theater. So it seems that Munchen is practically full of Germans and the lobby of the Kunst theater was really full of Germans who stand in the lobby and drink beer and eat quite a lot of Bermudian onions and garlick sausage and hard boiled eggs and beer before all of the acts. So I really had to ask Mr. Spoffard if he thought we had come to the right theatre because the lobby seemed to smell such a lot. I mean when the smell of beer gets to be anteek it gets to smell quite a lot. But Mr. Spoffard seemed to think that the lobby of the Kunst theatre did not smell any worse than all of the other places in Munich. So then Dorothy spoke up and Dorothy said "You can say what you want about the Germans being full of 'kunst,' but what they are really full of is delicatessen."

So then we went into the Kunst theater. But the Kunst theater does not seem to smell so good as the lobby of the Kunst theater. And the Kunst theater seems to be decorated with quite a lot of what tripe would look like if it was pasted on the wall and

115

gilded. Only you could not really see the gilding because it was covered with quite a lot of dust. So Dorothy looked around and Dorothy said, if this is "kunst," the art center of the world is Union Hill New Jersey.

So then they started in to playing Kiki but it seems that it was not the same kind of a Kiki that we have in America, because it seemed to be all about a family of large size German people who seemed to keep getting in each others ways. I mean when a stage is completely full of 2 or 3 German people who are quite large size, they really cannot help it if they seem to get in each others ways. So then Dorothy got to talking with a young gentleman who seemed to be a German gentleman who sat back of her, who she thought was applauding. But what he was really doing was he was cracking a hard boiled egg on the back of her chair. So he talked English with quite an accent that seemed to be quite a German accent. So Dorothy asked him if Kiki had come out on the stage yet. So he said no, but she was really a beautiful german actress who came clear from Berlin and he said we should really wait until she came out, even if we did not seem to understand it. So finally she came out. I mean we knew it was her because Dorothy's German gentleman friend nudged Dorothy with a sausage. So we looked at her, and we looked at her and Dorothy said, "If Schuman Heinke still has a grandmother, we have dug her up in Munchen." So we did not bother to see any more of Kiki because Dorothy said she would really have to know more about the foundations of that building before she would risk our lives to see Kiki do that famous scene where she faints in the last act. Because Dorothy said, if the foundations of that building were as anteek as the smell, there was going to be a catasterophy when Kiki hit the floor. So even Mr. Spoffard was quite discouradged, but he was really glad because he said he was 100 per cent. of an American and it served the Germans right for starting such a war against all we Americans.

May 20th:
Well today Mr. Spoffard is going to take me all around to all of the museums in Munchen, which are full of kunst that I really ought to look at, but Dorothy said she had been punished for all of her sins last night, so now she is going to begin life all over again by going out with her German gentleman friend, who is going to take her to a house called the Half Brow house which is the worlds largest size of a Beer Hall. So Dorothy said I could be a high brow and get full of kunst, but she is satisfide to be a Half brow and get full of beer. But Dorothy will really never be full of anything else but unrefinement.

May 21st:
Well Mr. Spoffard and I and Dorothy are on the train again and we are all going to Vienna. I mean Mr. Spoffard and I spent one whole day going through all of the museums in Munchen, but I am really not even going to think about it. Because when something terrible happens to me, I always try to be a Christian science and I simply do not even think about it, but I deny that it ever happened even if my feet do seem to hurt quite a lot. So even Dorothy had quite a hard day in Munchen because her German gentleman friend, who is called Rudolf, came for her at 11 oclock to take her to breakfast. But Dorothy told him that she had had her breakfast. But her gentleman friend said that he had had his first breakfast to, but it was time for his second. So he took Dorothy to the Half Brow house where everybody eats white sausages and pretzels and beer at 11 oclock. So after they had their white sausages and beer he wanted to take her for a ride but they could only go a few blocks because by then it was time for luncheon. So they ate quite a lot of luncheon and then he bought her a large size box of chocolates that were full of liqueurs, and took her to the matinee. So after the first act Rudolf got hungry and they had to go and stand in the lobby and have some sandwitches and beer. But Dorothy did not enjoy the show very much and so after the second act Rudolf said they

would leave because it was time for tea anyway. So after quite a heavy tea, Rudolph asked her to dinner and Dorothy was to overcome to say No. So after dinner they went to a beer garden for beer and pretzels. But finally Dorothy began to come to, and she asked him to take her back to the hotel. So Rudolf said he would, but they had better have a bite to eat first. So today Dorothy really feels just as discouradged as I seem to feel, only Dorothy is not a Christian science and all she can do is suffer.

But in spite of all of my Christian science, I am really beginning to feel quite discouradged about Vienna. I mean Mr. Eisman is in Vienna, and I do not see how I can spend quite a lot of time with Mr. Eisman and quite a lot of time with Mr. Spoffard and keep them from meeting one another. Because Mr. Spoffard might not seem to understand why Mr. Eisman seems to spend quite a lot of money to get me educated. And Dorothy keeps trying to depress me about Miss Chapman because she says she thinks that when Miss Chapman sees I and Mr. Spoffard together she thinks that Miss Chapman will cable for the familys favorite lunacy expert. So I have got to be as full of Christian science as I can and always hope for the best.

May 25th:
So far everything has really worked out for the best. Because Mr. Eisman is very very busy all day with the button profession, and he tells me to run around with Dorothy all day. So I and Mr. Spoffard run around all day. So then I tell Mr. Spoffard that I really do not care to go to all of the places that you go to at night, but I will go to bed and get ready for tomorrow instead. So then Dorothy and I go to dinner with Mr. Eisman and then we go to a show, and we stay up quite late at a cabaret called the Chapeau Rouge and I am able to keep it all up with the aid of champagne. So if we keep our eye out for Mr. Spoffard and do not all bump into one another when he is out looking at things that we Americans really should not look at, it will all work out for the best. I mean I have even stopped Mr. Spoffard looking at

museums because I tell him that I like nature better, and when you look at nature you look at it in a horse and buggy in the park and it is much easier on the feet. So now he is beginning to talk about how he would like me to meet his mother, so everything really seems for the best after all.

But I have quite a hard time with Mr. Eisman at night. I mean at night Mr. Eisman is in quite a state, because every time he makes an engagement about the button factory, it is time for all the gentlemen in Vienna to go to the coffee house and sit. Or else every time he makes an engagement about the button factory, some Viennese gentleman gets the idea to have a picknick and they all put on short pants and bare knees and they all put a feather in their hat, and they all walk to the Tyrol. So it really discouradges Mr. Eisman quite a lot. But if anyone ought to get discouradged I think that I ought to get discouradged because after all when a girl has had no sleep for a week a girl can not help it if she seems to get discouradged.

May 27th:

Well finaly I broke down and Mr. Spoffard said that he thought a little girl like I, who was trying to reform the whole world was trying to do to much, especially beginning on a girl like Dorothy. So he said there was a famous doctor in Vienna called Dr. Froyd who could stop all of my worrying because he does not give a girl medicine but he talks you out of it by psychoanalysis. So yesterday he took me to Dr. Froyd. So Dr. Froyd and I had quite a long talk in the english landguage. So it seems that everybody seems to have a thing called inhibitions, which is when you want to do a thing and you do not do it. So then you dream about it instead. So Dr. Froyd asked me, what I seemed to dream about. So I told him that I never really dream about anything. I mean I use my brains so much in the day time that at night they do not seem to do anything else but rest. So Dr. Froyd was very very surprized at a girl who did not dream about anything.

"Dr. Froyd seemed to think that I was quite a famous case."

So then he asked me all about my life. I mean he is very very sympathetic, and he seems to know how to draw a girl out quite a lot. I mean I told him things that I really would not even put in my diary. So then he seemed very very intreeged at a girl who always seemed to do everything she wanted to do. So he asked me if I really never wanted to do a thing that I did not do. For instance did I ever want to do a thing that was really vialent, for instance, did I ever want to shoot someone for instance. So then I said I had, but the bullet only went in Mr. Jennings lung and came right out again. So then Dr. Froyd looked at me and looked at me and he said he did not really think it was possible. So then he called in his assistance and he pointed at me and talked to his assistance quite a lot in the Viennese landguage. So then his assistance looked at me and looked at me and it really seems as if I was quite a famous case. So then Dr. Froyd said that all I needed was to cultivate a few inhibitions and get some sleep.

May 29th:
Things are really getting to be quite a strain. Because yesterday Mr. Spoffard and Mr. Eisman were both in the lobby of the Bristol hotel and I had to pretend not to see both of them. I mean it is quite an easy thing to pretend not to see one gentleman, but it is a quite hard thing to pretend not to see two gentlemen. So something has really got to happen soon, or I will have to admit that things seem to be happening that are not for the best.

So this afternoon Dorothy and I had an engagement to meet Count Salm for tea at four o'clock, only you do not call it tea at Vienna but you seem to call it "yowzer" and you do not drink tea at Vienna but you drink coffee instead. I mean it is quite unusual to see all of the gentlemen at Vienna stop work, to go to yowzer about one hour after they have all finished their luncheon, but time really does not seem to mean so much to Viennese gentlemen except time to get to the coffee house, which they all seem to know by instincts, or else they really do not seem to mind if they make a mistake and get there to early. Because Mr. Eisman says that when it is time to attend to the button profession, they really seem to lose all of their interest until Mr. Eisman is getting so nervous he could scream.

So we went to Deimels and met Count Salm. But while we were having yowzer with Count Salm, we saw Mr. Spoffard's mother come in with her companion Miss Chapman, and Miss Chapman seemed to look at me quite a lot and talk to Mr. Spoffards mother about me quite a lot. So I became quite nervous, because I really wished that we were not with Count Salm. I mean it has been quite a hard thing to make Mr. Spoffard think that I am trying to reform Dorothy, but if I had to try to make him think that I was trying to reform Count Salm, he might begin to think that there is a limit to almost everything. So Mr. Spoffards mother seems to be deaf, because she seems to use an ear trumpet and I really could not help over hearing quite a lot of words that Miss Chapman was using on me, even if it is not such good etiquet to overhear people. So Miss Chapman seemed to be telling Mr. Spoffards mother that I was a "creature," and she seemed to be telling her that I was the real reason why her son seemed to be so full of nothing but neglect lately. So then Mr. Spoffards mother looked at me and looked at me, even if it was not such good etiquet to look at a person. And Miss Chapman kept right on talking to Mr. Spoffards mother and I heard her mention Willie Gwynn and I think that Miss Chapman has been making some inquiries about me and I really think that she has heard about the time when all of the family of Willie Gwynn had quite a long talk with me and persuaded me not to marry Willie Gwynn for $10,000. So I really wish Mr. Spoffard would introduce me to his mother before she gets to be full of quite a lot of prejudice. Because one thing seems to be piling up on top of another thing, until I am almost on the verge of getting nervous and I have not had any time yet to do what Dr. Froyd said a girl ought to do. So tonight I am going to tell Mr. Eisman that I have got to go to bed early, so then I can take quite a long ride with Mr. Spoffard and look at nature, and he may say something definite, because nothing makes gentlemen get so definite as looking at nature when it is moonlight.

May 30th:

Well last night Mr. Spoffard and I took quite a long ride in the park, but they do not call it a park in the Viennese landguage but they call it the Prater. So a prater is really devine because it is just like Coney Island but at the same time it is in the woods and it is practically full of trees and it has quite a long road for people to take rides on in a horse and buggy. So I found out that Miss Chapman had been talking against me quite a lot. So it seems that she has been making inquiries about me, and I was really surprised to hear all of the things that Miss Chapman seemed to find out about me except that she did not find out about Mr. Eisman educating me. So then I had to tell Mr. Spoffard that I was not always so reformed as I am now, because the world was full of gentlemen who were nothing but wolfs in sheeps clothes, that did nothing but take advantadge of all we girls. So I really cried quite a lot. So then I told him how I was just a little girl from Little Rock when I first left Little Rock and by that time even Mr. Spoffard had tears in his eyes. So I told him how I came from a very very good family because papa was very intelectual, and he was a very very prominent Elk, and everybody always said that he was a very intelectual Elk. So I told Mr. Spoffard that when I left Little Rock I thought that all of the gentlemen did not want to do anything but protect we girls and by the time I found out that they did not want to protect us so much, it was to late. So then he cried quite a lot. So then I told him how I finaly got reformed by reading all about him in the newspapers and when I saw him in the oriental express it really seemed to be nothing but the result of fate. So I told Mr. Spoffard that I thought a girl was really more reformed if she knew what it was to be unreformed than if she was born reformed and never really knew that was the matter with her. So then Mr. Spoffard reached over and he kissed me on the forehead in a way that was full of reverance and he said I seemed to remind him quite a lot of a girl who got quite a write-up in the bible who was called Magdellen. So then he said that he used to be a member of the choir himself, so who was he to cast the first rock at a girl like I.

So we rode around in the Prater until it was quite late and it really was devine because it was moonlight and we talked quite a lot about morals, and all the bands in the prater were all playing in the distants "Mama love Papa". Because "Mama love Papa" has just reached Vienna and they all seem to be crazy about "Mama love Papa" even if it is not so new in America. So then he took me home to the hotel.

So everything always works out for the best, because this morning Mr. Spoffard called up and told me he wanted me to meet his mother. So I told him I would like to have luncheon alone with his mother because we could have quite a little tatatate if there was only two of us. So I told him to bring his mother to our room for luncheon because I thought that Miss Chapman could not walk into our room and spoil everything.

So he brought his mother down to our sitting room and I put on quite a simple little organdy gown that I had ripped all of the trimming off of, and I had a pair of black lace mitts that Dorothy used to wear in the Follies and I had a pair of shoes that did not have any heels on them. So when he introduced us to each other I dropped her a courtesy because I always think it is quite quaint when a girl drops quite a lot of courtesys. So then he left us alone and we had quite a little talk and I told her that I did not seem to like all of the flappers that we seem to have nowadays, because I was brought up to be more old fashioned. So then Mr. Spoffards mother told me that Miss Chapman said that she had heard that I was not so old fashioned. But I told her that I was so old fashioned that I was always full of respect for all of my elders and I would not dare to tell them everything they ought to do, like Miss Chapman seems to tell her everything she ought to do, for instants.

*"I told Mr. Spoffard's mother that I did not seem
to like all of the flappers we seem to have nowadays."*

125

So then I ordered luncheon and I thought some champagne would make her feel quite good for luncheon so I asked her if she liked champagne. So she really likes champagne very very much but Miss Chapman thinks it is not so nice for a person to drink liquor. But I told her that I was a Christian science, and all of we Christian science seem to believe that there can not really be any harm in anything, so how can there be any harm in a small size bottle of champagne? So she never seemed to look at it in that kind of a light before, because she said that Miss Chapman believed in Christian science also, but what Miss Chapman believed about things that were good for you to drink seemed to apply more towards water. So then we had luncheon and she began to feel very very good. So I thought that we had better have another bottle of champagne because I told her that I was such an ardent Christian science that I did not even believe there could be any harm in two bottles of champagne. So we had another bottle of champagne and she became very intreeged about Christian science because she said that she really thought it was a better religion than Prespyterians. So she said Miss Chapman used to try to get her to use it on things, but Miss Chapman never seemed to have such a large size grasp of the Christian science religion as I seem to have.

So then I told her that I thought Miss Chapman was jealous of her good looks. So then she said that that was true, because Miss Chapman would always make her wear hats that were made out of black horses hair because horses hair does not weigh so much on a persons brain. So I told her I was going to give her one of my hats that has got quite large size roses on it. So then I got it out, but we could not get it on her head because hats are quite small on account of hair being bobbed. So I thought I would get the sissors and bob her head, but then I thought I had done enough to her for one day.

So Henry's mother said that I was really the most sunshine that she ever had in all her life and when Henry came back to take his Mother up to her room, she did not want to go. But after he got her away he called me up on the telephone and he was qiute excited and he said he wanted to ask me something that was very very important. So I said I would see him tonight.

But now I have got to see Mr. Eisman because I have an idea about doing something that is really very very important that has got to be done at once.

May 31st:

Well I and Dorothy and Mr. Eisman are on a train going to a place called Buda Pest. So I did not see Henry again before I left, but I left him a letter. Because I thought it would be a quite good thing if what he wanted to ask me he would have to write down, instead of asking me, and he could not write it to me if I was in the same city that he is in. So I told him in my letter that I had to leave in five minute's time because I found out that Dorothy was just on the verge of getting very unreformed, and if I did not get her away, all I had done for her would really go for nothing. So I told him to write down what he had to say to me, and mail it to me at the Ritz hotel in Buda Pest. Because I always seem to believe in the old addage, Say it in writing.

So it was really very easy to get Mr. Eisman to leave Vienna, because yesterday he went out to see the button factory but it seems that all of the people at the button factory were not at work but they were giving a birthday party to some saint. So it seems that every time some saint has a birthday they all stop work so they can give it a birthday party. So Mr. Eisman looked at their calendar, and found out that some saint or other was born practically every week in the year. So he has decided that America is good enough for him.

So Henry will not be able to follow me to Buda Pest because his mother is having treatments by Dr. Froyd and she seems to be a much more difficult case than I seem to be. I mean it is quite hard for Dr. Froyd, because she cannot seem to remember which is a dream and which really happened to her. So she tells him everything, and he has to use his judgement. I mean when she tells him that a very very handsome young gentleman tried to flirt with her on Fifth Avenue, he uses his judgement.

So we will soon be at a Ritz hotel again and I must say it will be delightful to find a Ritz hotel right in the central of Europe.

June 1st:

Well yesterday Henrys letter came and it says in black and white that he and his mother have never met such a girl as I and he wants me to marry him. So I took Henrys letter to the photographers and I had quite a lot of photographs taken of it because a girl might lose Henrys letter and she would not have anything left to remember him by. But Dorothy says to hang on to Henry's letter, because she really does not think the photographs do it justice.

So this afternoon I got a telegram from Henry and the telegram says that Henry's father is very, very ill in New York and they have got to leave for New York immediately and his heart is broken not to see me again and to send him my answer by telegraph so that his mind will be rested while he is going back to New York. So I sent him a telegram and I accepted his proposal. So tonight I got another telegram and Henry says that he and his mother are very very happy and Henrys mother can hardly bear Miss Chapman any more and Henry says he hopes I will decide to come right back to New York and keep his mother quite a lot of company, because he thinks I can reform Dorothy more in New York anyway, where there is prohibition and nobody can get anything to drink.

So now I have got to make up my mind whether I really want to marry Henry after all. Because I know to much to get married to any gentleman like Henry without thinking it all over. Because Henry is the kind of a gentleman who gets on a girls nerves quite a lot and when a gentleman has nothing else to do but get on a girls nerves, there really seems to be a limit to almost everything. Because when a gentleman has a business, he has an office and he has to be there, but when a gentlemans business is only looking into other peoples business, a gentleman is always on the verge of coming in and out of the house. And a girl could not really say that her time was her own. And when Henry was not in and out of the house, his mother would always be in and out of the house because she seems to think that I am so full of nothing but sunshine. So it is quite a problem and I seem to be in quite a quarandary, because it might really be better if Henry should happen to decide that he should not get married, and he should change his mind, and desert a girl, and then it would only be right if a girl should sue him for a breach of promise.

But I really think, whatever happens, that Dorothy and I had better get back to New York. So I will see if Mr. Eisman will send us back. I mean I really do not think that Mr. Eisman will mind us going back because if he does, I will start shopping again and that always seems to bring him to terms. But all the time I am going back to New York, I will have to try to make up my mind one way or another. Because we girls really can not help it, if we have ideals, and sometimes my mind seems to get to running on things that are romantic, and I seem to think that maybe there is some place in the world where there is a gentleman who knows how to look and act like Count Salm and who has got money besides. And when a girls mind gets to thinking about such a romantic thing, a girls mind really does not seem to know whether to marry Henry or not.

CHAPTER SIX

BRAINS ARE REALLY EVERYTHING

June 14th:

Well, Dorothy and I arrived at New York yesterday because Mr. Eisman finally decided to send us home because he said that all of his button profession would not stand the strain of educating me much more in Europe. So we separated from Mr. Eisman in Buda Pest because Mr. Eisman had to go to Berlin to look up all of his starving relatives in Berlin, who have done nothing but starve since the War, so he wrote me just before we sailed and he said that he had dug up all his starving relatives and he had looked them all over, and decided not to bring them to America because there was not one of his starving relatives who could travel on a railroad ticket without paying excess fare for overweight.

So Dorothy and I took the boat and all the way over on the boat I had to make up my mind whether I really wanted to marry the famous Henry H. Spoffard, or not, because he was waiting for me to arrive at New York and he was so impatient that he could hardly wait for me to arrive at New York. But I have not wasted all of my time on Henry, even if I do not marry him, because I have some letters from Henry which would come in very, very handy if I did not marry Henry. So Dorothy seems to agree with me quite a lot, because Dorothy says the only thing she could stand being to Henry, would be to be his widow at the age of 18.

So coming over on the boat I decided not to bother to meet

any gentleman, because what good does it do to meet gentlemen when there is nothing to do on a boat but go shopping at a little shop where they do not have any thing that costs more than five dollars. And besides if I did meet any gentleman on the boat, he would want to see me off the boat, and then we would bump into Henry. But then I heard that there was a gentleman on the boat who was quite a dealer in unset diamonds from a town called Amsterdam. So I met the gentleman, and we went around together quite a lot, but we had quite a quarrel the night before we landed, so I did not even bother to look at him when I came down the gangplank, and I put the unset diamonds in my handbag so I did not have to declare them at the customs.

So Henry was waiting for me at the customs, because he had come up from Pennsylvania to meet me, because their country estate is at Pennsylvania, and Henry's father is very, very ill at Pennsylvania, so Henry has to stay there practically all of the time. So all of the reporters were at the customs and they all heard about how Henry and I were engaged to one another and they wanted to know what I was before I became engaged to Henry, so I told them that I was nothing but a society girl from Little Rock, Arkansas. So then I became quite angry with Dorothy because one of the reporters asked Dorothy when I made my debut in society at Little Rock and Dorothy said I made my debut at the Elks annual street fair and carnival at the age of 15, I mean Dorothy never overlooks any chance to be unrefined, even when she is talking to literary gentlemen like reporters.

So Henry brought me to the apartment in his Rolls Royce, and while we were coming to the apartment he said he wanted to give me my engagement ring and I really became all thrills. So he said that he had gone to Cartiers and he had looked over all the engagement rings in Cartiers and after he had looked them all over he had decided that they were not half good enough for me. So then he took a box out of his pocket and I really became intreeged. So then Henry said that when he looked at all of those large size diamonds he really felt that they did not have any sentiment, so he was going to give me his class ring from Amherst College insted. So then I looked at him and looked at him, but I am to full of self controle to say anything at this stage of the game, so I said it was really very sweet of him to be so full of nothing but sentiment.

So then Henry said that he would have to go back to Pennsylvania to talk to his father about us getting married, because his father has really got his heart set on us not getting married. So I told Henry that perhaps if I would meet his father, I would win him over, because I always seem to win gentlemen over. But Henry says that that is just the trouble, because some girl is always winning his father over, and they hardly dare to let him go out of their sight, and they hardly dare let him go to church alone. Because the last time he went to church alone some girl won him over on the street corner and he arrived back home with all of his pocket money gone, and they could not believe him when he said that he had put it in the plate, because he has not put more than a dime in the plate for the last fifty years.

So it seems that the real reason why his father does not want Henry to marry me, is because his father says that Henry always has all of the fun, and every time Henry's father wants to have some fun of his own, Henry always stops him and Henry will not even let him be sick at a hospital where he could have some fun of his own, but he keeps him at home where he has to have a nurse Henry picked out for him who is a male nurse. So all of his objections seem to be nothing but the spirit of resiprosity. But Henry says that all his objections cannot last much longer because he is nearly 90 years of age after all, and Nature must take its course sooner or later.

So Dorothy says what a fool I am to waste my time on Henry, when I might manage to meet Henry's father and the whole thing would be over in a few months and I would practically own the state of Pennsylvania.

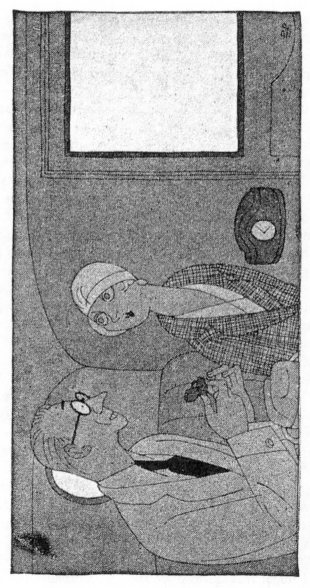

*"I told him that it was really very sweet
of him to be so full of nothing but sentiment."*

But I do not think I ought to take Dorothy's advise because Henry's father is watched like a hawk and Henry himself is his Power of Attorney, so no good could really come of it after all. And, after all, why should I listen to the advise of a girl like Dorothy who travelled all over Europe and all she came home with was a bangle!

So Henry spent the evening at the apartment and then he had to go back to Pennsylvania to be there Thursday morning, because every Thursday morning he belongs to a society who do nothing but senshure all of the photoplays. So they cut out all of the pieces out of all the photoplays that show things that are riskay, that people ought not to look at. So then they put all of the riskay pieces together and they run them over and over again. So it would really be quite a hard thing to drag Henry away from one of his Thursday mornings and he can hardly wait from one Thursday morning to another. Because he really does not seem to enjoy anything so much as senshuring photoplays and after a photoplay has once been senshured he seems to lose all of his interest in it.

So after Henry left I held quite a conversation with Lulu, who is my maid who looked out for my apartment while I was away. So Lulu really thinks I ought to marry Mr. Spoffard after all, because Lulu says that she kept studying Mr. Spoffard all of the time she was unpacking my trunks, and Lulu says she is sure that any time I feel as if I had to get away from Mr. Spoffard I could just set him down on the floor, and give him a packet of riskay french postcards to senshure and stay away as long as I like.

So Henry is going to arrange for me to come down to Pennsylvania for a week-end and meet all of his family. But if all of Henry's family are as full of reforms as Henry seems to be, it will be quite an ordeal even for a girl like I.

June 15th:
Yesterday morning was quite an ordeal for a refined girl because all of the newspapers all printed the story of how Henry

and I are engaged to one another, but they all seemed to leave out the part about me being a society girl except one newspaper, and that was the newspaper that quoted what Dorothy said about me being a debutant at the Elk's Carnival. So I called up Dorothy at the Ritz and I told Dorothy that a girl like she ought to keep her mouth closed in the presents of reporters.

So it seems that quite a lot of reporters kept calling Dorothy up but Dorothy said she really did not say anything to any of them except one reporter asked her what I used for money and she told him buttons. But Dorothy really should not have said such a thing, because quite a few people seem to know that Mr. Eisman is educating me and that he is known all over Chicago as Gus Eisman the Button King, so one thing might suggest another until people's minds might begin to think something.

But Dorothy said that she did not say anything more about me being a debutant at Little Rock, because after all Dorothy knows that I really did not make any debut in Little Rock, because just when it was time to make my debut, my gentleman friend Mr. Jennings became shot, and after the trial was over and all of the Jury had let me off, I was really much to fatigued to make any debut.

So then Dorothy said, why don't we throw a party now and you can become a debutant now and put them all in their place, because it seems that Dorothy is dying for a party. So that is really the first sensible suggestion that Dorothy has made yet, because I think that every girl who is engaged to a gentleman who has a fine old family like Henry, had really ought to be a debutant. So I told her to come right over and we would plan my debut but we would keep it very, very quiet and give it tomorrow night, because if Henry heard I was making my debut he would come up from Pennsylvania and he would practically spoil the party, because all Henry has to do to spoil a party is to arrive at it.

So Dorothy came over and we planned my debut. So first we decided to have some engraved invitations engraved, but it always takes quite a little time to have invitations engraved, and it would really be foolish because all of the gentlemen we were going to invite to my debut were all members of the Racquet Club, so I could just write out a notice that I was having a debut and give it to Willie Gwynn and have Willie Gwynn post it on the Racquet Club board.

So Willie Gwynn posted it on the club board and then he called me up and he told me that he had never seen so much enthusiasm since the Dempsey-Firpo fight, and he said that the whole Racquet Club would be there in a body. So then we had to plan about what girls we would ask to my debut. Because I have not seemed to meet so many society women yet because of course a girl does not meet society women until her debut is all over, and then all the society women all come and call on a debutant. But I know practically all of the society men, because practically all of the society men belong to the Racquet club, so after I have the Racquet Club at my debut, all I have to do to take my real place in society is to meet their mothers and sisters, because I know practically all of their sweethearts now.

But I always seem to think that it is delightful to have quite a lot of girls at a party, if a girl has quite a lot of gentlemen at a party, and it is quite delightful to have all the girls from the Follies, but I really could not invite them because, after all, they are not in my set. So then I thought it all over and I thought that even if it was not etiquette to invite them to a party, it really would be etiquette to hire them to come to a party and be entertainers, and after they were entertainers they could mix in to the party and it really would not be a social error.

So then the telephone rang and Dorothy answered it and it seems that it was Joe Sanguinetti, who is almost the official bootlegger for the whole Racquet Club, and Joe said he had heard about my debut and if he could come to my debut and bring his club which is the Silver Spray Social Club of Brooklyn, he would supply all of the liquor and he would guarantee to practically run the rum fleet up to the front door.

So Dorothy told him he could come, and she hung up the telephone before she told me his proposition, and I became quite angry with Dorothy because, after all, the Silver Spray Social Club is not even mentioned in the Social Register and it has no place at a girl's debut. But Dorothy said by the time the party got into swing, anyone would have to be a genius if he could tell whether he belonged to the Racquet Club, the Silver Spray Social Club, or the Knights of Pythias. But I really was almost sorry that I asked Dorothy to help plan my debut, except that Dorothy is very good to have at a party if the police come in, because Dorothy always knows how to manage the police, and I never knew a policeman yet who did not finish up by being madly in love with Dorothy. So then Dorothy called up all of the reporters on all of the newspapers and invited them all to my debut, so they could see it with their own eyes.

So Dorothy says that she is going to see to it that my debut lands on the front page of all of the newspapers, if we have to commit a murder to do it.

June 19th:

Well, it has been three days since my debut party started but I finally got tired and left the party last night and went to bed because I always seem to lose all of my interest in a party after a few days, but Dorothy never loses her interest in a party and when I woke up this morning Dorothy was just saying goodbye to some of the guests. I mean Dorothy seems to have quite a lot of vitality, because the last guests of the party were guests we picked up when the party went to take a swim at Long Beach the day before yesterday, and they were practically fresh, but Dorothy had gone clear through the party from beginning to end without even stopping to go to a Turkish bath as most of the gentlemen had to do. So my debut has really been very novel, because quite a lot of the guests who finished up at my debut were not the same guests that started out at it, and it is really quite novel for a girl to have so many different kinds of gentlemen at

her debut. So it has really been a very great success because all of
the newspapers have quite a lot of write-ups about my debut and
I really felt quite proud when I saw the front page of the *Daily
Views* and it said in large size headlines, "LORELEI'S DEBUT
A WOW!" And *Zits' Weekly* came right out and said that if
this party marks my entrance into society, they only hope that
they can live to see what I will spring once I have overcome my
debutant reserve and taken my place in the world.

So I really had to apologise to Dorothy about asking Joe
Sanguinetti to my debut because it was wonderful the way he
got all of the liquor to the party and he more than kept his
word. I mean he had his bootleggers run up from the wharf in
taxis, right to the apartment, and the only trouble he had was,
that once the bootleggers delivered the liquor, he could not get
them to leave the party. So finally there was quite a little quarrel
because Willie Gwynn claimed that Joe's bootleggers were
snubbing the members of his club because they would not let
the boys from the Racquet club sing in their quartet. But Joe's
bootleggers said that the Racquet club boys wanted to sing
songs that were unrefined, while they wanted to sing songs
about Mother. So then everybody started to take sides, but the
girls from the Follies were all with Joe's bootleggers from the
start because practically all we girls were listening to them with
tears steaming from our eyes. So that made the Racquet club
jealous and one thing led to another until somebody rang for an
ambulants and then the police came in.

So Dorothy, as usual, won over all of the police. So it seems
that the police all have orders from Judge Schultzmeyer, who
is the famous judge who tries all of the prohibition cases, that
any time they break into a party that looks like it was going to
be a good party, to call him up no matter what time of the day
or night it is, because Judge Schultzmeyer dearly loves a party.
So the Police called up Judge Schultzmeyer and he was down
in less than no time. So during the party both Joe Sanguinetti
and Judge Schultzmeyer fell madly in love with Dorothy. So Joe

and the Judge had quite a little quarrel and the Judge told Joe that if his stuff was fit to drink he would set the Law after him and confiscate it, but his stuff was not worth the while of any gentleman to confiscate who had any respect for his stomach, and he would not lower himself to confiscate it. So along about nine o'clock in the morning Judge Schultzmeyer had to leave the party and go to court to try all of the criminals who break all of the laws, so he had to leave Dorothy and Joe together and he was very very angry. And I really felt quite sorry for any person who went up before Judge Schultzmeyer that morning, because he gave everybody 90 days and was back at the party by twelve o'clock. So then he stuck to the party until we were all going down to Long Beach to take a swim day before yesterday when he seemed to become unconscious, so we dropped him off at a sanitorium in Garden City.

So my debut party was really the greatest success of the social season, because the second night of my debut party was the night when Willie Gwynn's sister was having a dance at the Gwynn estate on Long Island, and Willie Gwynn said that all of the eligible gentlemen in New York were conspicuous by their absents at his sister's party, because they were all at my party. So it seems as if I am really going to be quite a famous hostess if I can just bring my mind to the point of being Mrs. Henry Spoffard Jr.

Well Henry called up this morning and Henry said he had finally got his father's mind so that he thought it was safe for me to meet him and he was coming up to get me this afternoon so that I can meet his family and see his famous old historical home at Pennsylvania. So then he asked about my debut party which some of the Philadelphia papers seemed to mention. But I told him that my debut was really not so much planned, as it was spontaneous, and I did not have the heart to call him up at a moments notice and take him away from his father at such a time for reasons which were nothing but social.

"My debut was the greatest success of the social season."

So now I am getting ready to visit Henry's family and I feel as if my whole future depends on it. Because if I can not stand Henry's family any more than I can stand Henry the whole thing will probly come to an end in the law court.

June 21st:
Well, I am now spending the weekend with Henry's family at his old family mansion outside of Philadelphia, and I am beginning to think, after all, that there is something else in the world besides family. And I am beginning to think that family life is only fit for those who can stand it. For instants, they always seem to get up very early in Henry's family. I mean it really is not so bad to get up early when there is something to get up early about, but when a girl gets up early and there is nothing to get up early about, it really begins to seem as if there was no sense to it.

So yesterday we all got up early and that was when I met all of Henry's family, because Henry and I motored down to Pennsylvania and everybody was in bed when we arrived because it was after nine o'clock. So in the morning Henry's mother came to my room to get me up in time for breakfast because Henry's mother is very very fond of me, and she always wants to copy all of my gowns and she always loves to look through all of my things to see what I have got. So she found a box of liqueur candies that are full of liqueurs and she was really very delighted. So I finally got dressed and she threw the empty box away and I helped her down stairs to the Dining room.

So Henry was waiting in the dining room with his sister and that was when I met his sister. So it seems that Henry's sister has never been the same since the war, because she never had on a man's collar and a necktie until she drove an ambulants in the war, and now they cannot get her to take them off. Because ever since the armistice Henry's sister seems to have the idea that regular womens clothes are effiminate. So Henry's sister seems to think of nothing but either horses or automobiles and

142

when she is not in a garage the only other place she is happy in is a stable. I mean she really pays very little attention to all of her family and she seems to pay less attention to Henry than anybody else because she seems to have the idea that Henry's brains are not so viril. So then we all waited for Henry's father to come in so that he could read the Bible out loud before breakfast.

So then something happened that really was a miracle. Because it seems that Henry's father has practically lived in a wheel chair for months and months and his male nurse has to wheel him everywhere. So his male nurse wheeled him into the dining room in his wheel chair and then Henry said "Father, this is going to be your little daughter in law," and Henry's father took one good look at me and got right out of his wheel chair and walked! So then everybody was very very surprised, but Henry was not so surprised because Henry knows his father like a book. So then they all tried to calm his father down, and his father tried to read out of the Bible but he could hardly keep his mind on the Bible and he could hardly eat a bite because when a gentleman is as feeble as Henry's father is, he cannot keep one eye on a girl and the other eye on his cereal and cream without coming to grief. So Henry finally became quite discouradged and he told his father he would have to get back to his room or he would have a relapse. So then the male nurse wheeled him back to his room and it really was pathetic because he cried like a baby. So I got to thinking over what Dorothy advised me about Henry's father and I really got to thinking that if Henry's father could only get away from everybody and have some time of his own, Dorothy's advise might not be so bad after all.

So after breakfast we all got ready to go to church, but Henry's sister does not go to church because Henry's sister always likes to spend every Sunday in the garage taking their Ford farm truck apart and putting it back together again, and Henry says that what the war did to a girl like his sister is really worse than the war itself.

143

*"Henry's father cannot keep one eye on a girl
and the other on his cereal without coming to grief."*

144

So then Henry and his mother and I all went to church. So we came home from church and we had luncheon and it seems that luncheon is practically the same as breakfast except that Henry's father could not come down to luncheon because after he met me he contracted such a vialent fever that they had to send for the Doctor.

So in the afternoon Henry went to prayer meeting and I was left alone with Henry's mother so that we could rest up so that we could go to church again after supper. So Henry's mother thinks I am nothing but sunshine and she will hardly let me get out of her sight, because she hates to be by herself because, when she is by herself, her brains hardly seem to work at all. So she loves to try on all of my hats and she loves to tell me how all the boys in the choir can hardly keep their eyes off her. So of course a girl has to agree with her, and it is quite difficult to agree with a person when you have to do it through an ear trumpet because sooner or later your voice has to give out.

So then supper turned out to be practically the same thing as luncheon only by supper time all of the novelty seemed to wear off. So then I told Henry that I had to much of a headache to go to church again, so Henry and his mother went to church and I went to my room and I sat down and thought and I decided that life was really to short to spend it in being proud of your family, even if they did have a great deal of money. So the best thing for me to do is to think up some scheme to make Henry decide not to marry me and take what I can get out of it and be satisfied.

June 22nd:

Well, yesterday I made Henry put me on the train at Philadelphia and I made him stay at Philadelphia so he could be near his father if his father seemed to take any more relapses. So I sat in my drawing room on the train and I decided that the time had come to get rid of Henry at any cost. So I decided that the thing that discouradges gentlemen more than anything else is shopping. Because even Mr. Eisman, who was practically born for we girls to shop on, and who knows just what to expect, often gets quite discouradged over all of my shopping. So I decided I would get to New York and I would go to Cartiers and run up quite a large size bill on Henry's credit, because after all our engagement has been announced in all of the newspapers, and Henry's credit is really my credit.

So while I was thinking it all over there was a knock on the drawing room door, so I told him to come in and it was a gentleman who said he had seen me quite a lot in New York and he had always wanted to have an introduction to me, because we had quite a lot of friends who were common. So then he gave me his card and his name was on his card and it was Mr. Gilbertson Montrose and his profession is a senario writer. So then I asked him to sit down and we held a literary conversation.

So I really feel as if yesterday was a turning point in my life, because at last I have met a gentleman who is not only an artist but who has got brains besides. I mean he is the kind of a gentleman that a girl could sit at his feet and listen to for days and days and nearly always learn something or other. Because, after all, there is nothing that gives a girl more of a thrill than brains in a gentleman, especially after a girl has been spending the week end with Henry. So Mr. Montrose talked and talked all of the way to New York and I sat there and did nothing else but listen. So according to Mr. Montrose's opinion Shakespear is a very great playwrite, and he thinks that Hamlet is quite a famous tragedy and as far as novels are concerned he believes that nearly everybody had ought to read Dickens. And when we got on the subject of poetry he recited "The Shooting of Dan McGrew" until you could almost hear the gun go off.

And then I asked Mr. Montrose to tell me all about himself. So it seems that Mr. Montrose was on his way home from Washington D. C., where he went to see the Bulgarian Ambassadore to see if he could get Bulgaria to finance a senario he has written which is a great historical subject which is founded on the sex life of Dolly Madison.

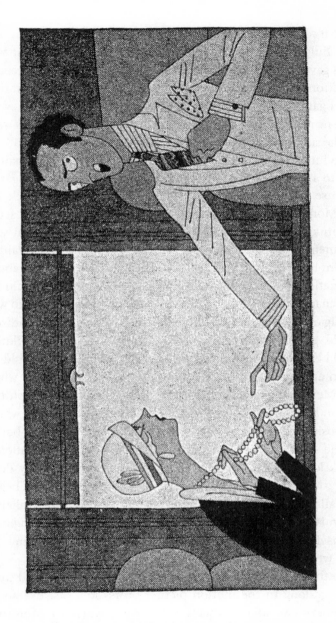

*"When he recited 'The Shooting of Dan McGrew'
you could almost hear the gun go off."*

So it seems that Mr. Montrose has met quite a lot of Bulgarians in a Bulgarian restaurant on Lexington Avenue and that was what gave him the idea to get the money from Bulgaria. Because Mr. Montrose said that he could fill his senario full of Bulgarian propoganda, and he told the Bulgarian Ambassadore that every time he realised how ignorant all of the American film fans were on the subject of Bulgaria, it made him flinch.

So I told Mr. Montrose that it made me feel very very small to talk to a gentleman like he, who knew so much about Bulgaria, because practically all I knew about Bulgaria was Zoolack. So Mr. Montrose said that the Bulgarian Ambassadore did not seem to think that Dolly Madison had so much about her that was pertinent to present day Bulgaria, but Mr. Montrose explained to him that that was because he knew practically nothing about dramatic construction. Because Mr. Montrose said he could fix his senario so that Dolly Madison would have one lover who was a Bulgarian, who wanted to marry her. So then Dolly Madison would get to wondering what her great, great grandchildren would be like if she married a Bulgarian, and then she could sit down and have a vision of Bulgaria in 1925. So that was when Mr. Montrose would take a trip to Bulgaria to photograph the vision. But the Bulgarian Ambassadore turned down the whole proposition, but he gave Mr. Montrose quite a large size bottle of the Bulgarian national drink. So the Bulgarian national drink looks like nothing so much as water, and it really does not taste so strong, but about five minutes afterwards you begin to realise your mistake. But I thought to myself that if realizing my mistake could make me forget what I went through in Pennsylvania, I really owed it to myself to forget everything. So then we had another drink.

So then Mr. Montrose told me that he had quite a hard time getting along in the motion picture profession, because all of his senarios are all over their head. Because when Mr. Montrose writes about sex, it is full of sychology, but when everybody else writes about it, it is full of nothing but transparent negligays and ornamental bath tubs. And Mr. Montrose says that there is no future in the motion pictures until the motion pictures get their sex motives straightened out, and realize that a woman of 25 can have just as many sex problems as a flapper of 16. Because Mr. Montrose likes to write about women of the world, and he refuses to have women of the world played by small size girls of 15 who know nothing about life and who have not even been in the detention home.

So we both arrived in New York before we realized it, and I got to thinking how the same trip with Henry in his Rolls Royce seemed like about 24 hours, and that was what gave me the idea that money was not everything, because after all, it is only brains that count. So Mr. Montrose took me home and we are going to have luncheon together at the Primrose Tea room practically every day and keep right on holding literary conversations.

So then I had to figure out how to get rid of Henry and at the same time not do anything that would make me any trouble later. So I sent for Dorothy because Dorothy is not so good at intreeging a gentleman with money, but she ought to be full of ideas on how to get rid of one.

So at first Dorothy said, Why didn't I take a chance and marry Henry because she had an idea that if Henry married me he would commit suicide about two weeks later. But I told her about my plan to do quite a lot of shopping, and I told her that I would send for Henry and I would manage it so that I would not be in the apartment when he came, but she could be there and start a conversation with him and she could tell him about all of my shopping and how extravagant I seemed to be and he would be in the poor house in less than a year if he married me.

So Dorothy said for me to take one farewell look at Henry and leave him to her, because the next time I saw him would be in the witness box and I might not even recognize him because she would throw a scare into him that might change his whole physical appearance. So I decided to leave him in the hands of Dorothy and hope for the best.

July 10th:
Well, last month was really almost a diary in itself, and I have to begin to realize that I am one of the kind of girls that things happen to. And I have to admit, after all, that life is really wonderful. Because so much has happened in the last few weeks that it almost makes a girl's brains whirl.

I mean in the first place I went shopping at Cartiers and bought quite a delightful square cut emerald and quite a long rope of pearls on Henry's credit. So then I called up Henry on the long distants telephone and told him that I wanted to see him quite a lot, so he was very very pleased and he said that he would come right up to New York.

So then I told Dorothy to come to the apartment and be there when Henry came, and to show Henry what I bought on his credit, and to tell him how extravagant I seem to be, and how I seem to keep on getting worse. So I told Dorothy to go as far as she liked, so long as she did not insinuate anything against my character, because the more spotless my character seems to be, the better things might turn out later. So Henry was due at the apartment about 1.20, so I had Lulu get some luncheon for he and Dorothy and I told Dorothy to tell him that I had gone out to look at the Russian Crown Jewels that some Russian Grand Duchess or other had for sale at the Ritz.

So then I went to the Primrose Tea Room to have luncheon with Mr. Montrose because Mr. Montrose loves to tell me of all his plans, and he says that I seem to remind him quite a lot of a girl called Madame Recamier who all the intelectual gentlemen used to tell all of their plans to, even when there was a French revolution going on all around them.

So Mr. Montrose and I had a delicious luncheon, except that I never seem to notice what I am eating when I am with Mr. Montrose because when Mr. Montrose talks a girl wants to do nothing but listen. But all of the time I was listening, I was thinking about Dorothy and I was worrying for fear Dorothy would go to far, and tell Henry something that would not be so good for me afterwards. So finally even Mr. Montrose seemed to notice it, and he said "What's the matter little woman, a penny for your thoughts."

So then I told him everything. So he seemed to think quite a lot and finally he said to me "It is really to bad that you feel as if the social life of Mr. Spoffard bored you, because Mr. Spoffard would be ideal to finance my senario." So then Mr. Montrose said that he had been thinking from the very first how ideal I would be to play Dolly Madison. So that started me thinking and I told Mr. Montrose that I expected to have quite a large size ammount of money later on, and I would finance it myself. But Mr. Montrose said that would be to late, because all of the motion picture corporations were after it now, and it would be snaped up almost immediately.

So then I became almost in a panick, because I suddenly decided that if I married Henry and worked in the motion pictures at the same time, society life with Henry would not really be so bad. Because if a girl was so busy as all that, it really would not seem to matter so much if she had to stand Henry when she was not busy. But then I realized what Dorothy was up to, and I told Mr. Montrose that I was almost afraid it was to late. So I hurried to the telephone and I called up Dorothy at the apartment and I asked her what she had said to Henry. So Dorothy said that she showed him the square cut emerald and told him that I bought it as a knick-knack to go with a green dress, but I had got a spot on the dress, so I was going to give them both to Lulu. So she said she showed him the pearls and she said that after I had bought them, I was sorry I did not get pink ones because white ones were so common, so I was going to have Lulu unstring them and sew them on a negligay. So then she told him she was rather sorry I meant to buy the Russian Crown jewels because she had a feeling they were unlucky, but that I had said to her, that if I found out they were, I could toss them over my left shoulder into the Hudson river some night when there was a new moon, and it would take away the curse.

So then she said that Henry began to get restless. So then she told him she was very glad I was going to get married at last because I had had such bad luck, that every time I became engaged something seemed to happen to my fiance. So Henry asked her what, for instance. So Dorothy said a couple were in the insane asylum, one had shot himself for debt, and the county farm was taking care of the remainder. So Henry asked her how they got that way. So Dorothy told him it was nothing but my extravagants, and she told him that she was surprised that he had never heard about it, because all I had to do was to take luncheon at the Ritz with some prominent broker and the next day the bottom would drop out of the market. And she told him that she did not want to insinuate anything, but that I had dined with a very, very prominent German the day before German marks started to colapse.

So I became almost frantic and I told Dorothy to hold Henry at the apartment until I could get up there and explain. So I held the telephone while Dorothy went to see if Henry would wait. So Dorothy came back in a minute and she said that the parlor was empty, but that if I would hurry down to Broadway no doubt I would see a cloud of dust heading towards the Pennsylvania station, and that would be Henry.

So then I went back to Mr. Montrose, and I told him that I must catch Henry at the Pennsylvania Station at any cost. And if anyone were to say that we left the Primrose tea room in a hurry, they would be putting it quite mildly. So we got to the Pennsylvania station and I just had time to get on board the train to Philadelphia and I left Mr. Montrose standing at the train biting his finger nails in all of his anxiety. But I called out to him to go to his Hotel and I would telephone the result as soon as the train arrived.

So then I went through the train, and there was Henry with a look on his face which I shall never forget. So when he saw me he really seemed to shrink to ½ his natural size. So I sat down beside him and I told him that I was really ashamed of how he acted, and if his love for me could not stand a little test that I and Dorothy had thought up, more in the spirit of fun than anything else, I never wanted to speak to such a gentleman again. And I told him that if he could not tell the difference between a real square cut emerald and one from the ten cent store, that he had ought to be ashamed of himself. And I told him that if he thought that every string of white beads were pearls, it was no wonder he could make such a mistake in judging the character of a girl. So then I began to cry because of all of Henry's lack of faith. So then he tried to cheer me up but I was to hurt to even give him a decent word until we were past Newark. But by the time we were past Newark, Henry was crying himself, and it always makes me feel so tender hearted to listen to a gentleman cry that I finally forgave him. So, of course, as soon as I got home I had to take them back to Cartiers.

So then I explained to Henry how I wanted our life to mean something and I wanted to make the World a better place than it seemed to have been yet. And I told him that he knew so much about the film profession on account of senshuring all of the films that I thought he had ought to go into the film profession. Because I told him that a gentleman like he really owed it to the world to make pure films so that he could be an example to all of the other film corporations and show the world what pure films were like. So Henry became very, very intreeged because he had never thought of the film profession before. So then I told him that we could get H. Gilbertson Montrose to write the senarios, and he to senshure them, and I could act in them and by the time we all got through, they would be a work of art. But they would even be purer than most works of art seem to be. So by the time we got to Philadelphia Henry said that he would do it, but he really did not think I had ought to act in them. But I told him from what I had seen of society women trying to break into the films, I did not believe that it would be so declasée if one of them really landed. So I even talked him into that.

So when we got to Henry's country estate, we told all of

Henry's family and they were all delighted. Because it is the first time since the war that Henry's family have had anything definite to put their minds on. I mean Henry's sister really jumped at the idea because she said she would take charge of the studio trucks and keep them at a bed-rock figure. So I even promised Henry's mother that she could act in the films. I mean I even believe that we could put in a close-up of her from time to time, because after all, nearly every photoplay has to have some comedy relief. And I promised Henry's father that we would wheel him through the studio and let him look at all of the actresses and he nearly had another relapse. So then I called up Mr. Montrose and made an appointment with him to meet Henry and talk it all over, and Mr. Montrose, said, "Bless you, little woman."

So I am almost beginning to believe it, when everybody says I am nothing but sunshine because everybody I come into contract with always seems to become happy. I mean with the exception of Mr. Eisman. Because when I got back to New York, I opened all of his cablegrams and I realized that he was due to arrive on the *Aquitania* the very next day. So I met him at the *Aquitania* and I took him to luncheon at the Ritz and I told him all about everything. So then he became very, very depressed because he said that just as soon as he had got me all educated, I had to go off and get married. But I told him that he really ought to be very proud of me, because in the future, when he would see me at luncheon at the Ritz as the wife of the famous Henry H. Spoffard, I would always bow to him, if I saw him, and he could point me out to all of his friends and tell them that it was he, Gus Eisman himself, who educated me up to my station. So that cheered Mr. Eisman up a lot and I really do not care what he says to his friends, because, after all, his friends are not in my set, and whatever he says to them will not get around in my circle. So after our luncheon was all over, I really think that, even if Mr. Eisman was not so happy, he could not help having a sort of a feeling of relief, especially when he thinks of all my shopping.

So after that came my wedding and all of the Society people in New York and Philadelphia came to my wedding and they were all so sweet to me, because practically every one of them has written a senario. And everybody says my wedding was very, very beautiful. I mean even Dorothy said it was very beautiful, only Dorothy said she had to concentrate her mind on the massacre of the Armenians to keep herself from laughing right out loud in everybody's face. But that only shows that not even Matrimony is sacred to a girl like Dorothy. And after the wedding was over, I overheard Dorothy talking to Mr. Montrose and she was telling Mr. Montrose that she thought that I would be great in the movies if he would write me a part that only had three expressions, Joy, Sorrow, and Indigestion. So I do not really believe that Dorothy is such a true friend after all.

So Henry and I did not go on any honeymoon because I told Henry that it really would be selfish for us to go off alone together, when all of our activities seemed to need us so much. Because, after all, I have to spend quite a lot of time with Mr. Montrose going over the senario together because, Mr. Montrose says I am full of nothing so much as ideas.

So, in order to give Henry something to do while Mr. Montrose and I are working on the senario I got Henry to organize a Welfare League among all of the extra girls and get them to tell him all of their problems so he can give them all of his spiritual aid. And it has really been a very, very great success, because there is not much work going on at the other studios at present so all of the extra girls have nothing better to do and they all know that Henry will not give them a job at our studio unless they belong. So the worse they tell Henry they have been before they met him, the better he likes it and Dorothy says that she was at the studio yesterday and she says that if the senarios those extra girls have written around themselves to tell Henry could only be screened and gotten past the sensors, the movies would move right up out of their infancy.

So Henry says that I have opened up a whole new world for

him and he has never been so happy in his life. And it really seems as if everyone I know has never been so happy in their lives. Because I make Henry let his father come to the studio every day because, after all, every studio has to have somebody who seems to be a pest, and in our case it might just as well be Henry's father. So I have given orders to all of the electricians not to drop any lights on him, but to let him have a good time because, after all, it is the first one he has had. And as far as Henry's mother is concerned, she is having her hair bobbed and her face lifted and getting ready to play Carmen because she saw a girl called Madam Calve play it when she was on her honeymoon and she has always really felt that she could do it better. So I do not discouradge her, but I let her go ahead and enjoy herself. But I am not going to bother to speak to the electricians about Henry's mother. And Henry's sister has never been so happy since the Battle of Verdun, because she has six trucks and 15 horses to look after and she says that the motion picture profession is the nearest thing to war that she has struck since the Armistice. And even Dorothy is very happy because Dorothy says that she has had more laughs this month than Eddie Cantor gets in a year. But when it comes to Mr. Montrose, I really believe that he is happier than anybody else, because of all of the understanding and sympathy he seems to get out of me.

And so I am very happy myself because, after all, the greatest thing in life is to always be making everybody else happy. And so, while everybody is so happy, I really think it is a good time to finish my diary because after all, I am to busy going over my senarios with Mr. Montrose, to keep up any other kind of literary work. And I am so busy bringing sunshine into the life of Henry that I really think, with everything else I seem to acomplish, it is all a girl had ought to try to do. And so I really think that I can say good-bye to my diary feeling that, after all, everything always turns out for the best.